THE 100 STEPS NECESSARY

for

SURVIVAL™

on the

EARTH

RM Soccolich

*The 100 Steps Necessary
for Survival on the Earth*
is published by:

SEABURN
"Books for the Open Mind"

Copyright © 1992 by RM Soccolich

ISBN: 1-885778-05-8

Library of Congress Cat. Num. in publication data

For information on the *Survival Series* call:
(718) 274-1300

Seaburn Publishing
PO Box 2085
Astoria, NY 11102

1

REALITY, through its selfsame, sub-atomic particle activity is consistently changing and recreating itself. Therefore, rewrite the novel of your existence with each passing moment of each and every day.

I know this is a 'heavy-handed' first step, but bare with me; it'll be over soon... There is an unmistakable connection between our physical self (body) and our psychological self (mind). Hence, our perception of the world has to be as flexible and pliable as the outside or physical world itself. We note that the material earth in which we live can be broken down into finite sub-atomic particles. Quantum physics demonstrates how these minuscule building blocks of matter undergo constant transitions and random changes. In fact, these sub-atomic particles change aspects of their 'position' and 'purpose' each time physicists attempt to focus upon their exact nature. This scientific dilemma has been coined: "The Uncertainty Principle", and has shaken hard science to its very foundations. In other words, reality is in flux and hasn't stated its exact 'plan' as of yet. Now, does this leave us with the absolute philosophical premise that we need to recreate ourselves each and every passing moment of our lives like some surreal Tibetan monk? You bet your American bottom it does! As human beings, we simply need to utilize our mental flexibility in order to approach each new situation of an ever-creating reality with some semblance of reasonable truth.

AVOID what you instantly recognize. All inclusive familiarity is brain death.

As human beings, we find comfort in familiar sights and sounds. (Goo Goo.) We are not threatened by people or objects who we have come to know and understand over time. However, strangers and new situations tend to uproot our normal levels of confidence. Boo! Boo!!! As society continues to grow, we find ourselves further and further enmeshed in an unfamiliar terrain replete with new faces and novel concepts. In order to remain successful in these rapidly changing times, we must accept and embrace the unknown. As we tackle our preconceived prejudices we will begin to dissolve our irrational fears. Conversely, if we remain fixated in a familiar environment we will only limit our rational ability to learn and grow as human beings within a civilized society.
(And face it, that would be stupid...)

DROP all titles you've ever known. Titles and categories are waste products of a power hungry forebrain.

As a society, we use titles and categories to simplify our abstract understanding of individual human works of art and science. (Ex: "What sort of a book is this, son?") Furthermore, we use titles to group these works into organized catalogues of information. ("Oh, that kind of book.") On the surface, this system of classification seems effective in a world of rapidly expanding data. However, when we replace the complex understanding of a unique work in favor of the general comprehension which its category offers, we lose sight of the works singular meaning and original message. (Oh, its THAT THERE kind of book!") This oversimplification effects the work's observer as well as the work's creator who must formulate his vision to coincide with a 'title category' and all its subsequent expectations. (Well...its like one of those books, but...) MUST WE let categorization Divide and Conquer the intricate, complex and multifaceted human mind? Hell no! In any case, as individuals, we may need to surpass a work's classification and judge its singular merits on our own unique terms. This way we'll really see what's OUT THERE, one work at a time. Besides, who dares to SIMPLIFY your human brain?!!

4

DO not be fooled by the forebrain. Language is invisible. Do not 'see' objects as they are 'named', 'see' objects for what they are...shape, smoothness, color, texture...

Language is indeed a formidable tool. It promotes communication, comprehension and interactive society itself. However, language simply cannot replace the reality of our own five senses and their subtle and countless emotional reverberations. (Remember that time at the beach, when your hormones first kicked in?) Description assists our understanding of persons and objects, however as stated, nothing can take the place of real face to face human interaction. Keeping this tenet in mind, we may need to suspend our personal assessment (OF ALL!) persons and things until we have experienced their true presence first hand. (Like that time at the beach, when your hormones first kicked in?) People and objects vibrate at certain frequencies which may or may not harmonize with our own physiological impulses. This is why certain people, objects and situations may 'feel' absolutely 'wrong' to us. Conversely, our own positive vibrations can be sensed by the myriad of people who we personally come into contact with day in and day out. This factor, combined with some luck, may prevent these people from shooting you in the face with their assault rifles.

THE systematic elimination of nouns will enable the beginning of some true reality.

When we contemplate the use of a noun we are considering passive objects which have not been 'acted upon' by verbs. In this sense, we conceptualize nouns as frozen, lifeless realities awaiting some form of action (verb). (See the dog. What does the dog do? So far, the dog does nothing. The dog is either dead or really despondent.) Fortunately, nouns and verbs are physically inseparable since matter is constantly undergoing random changes (see Step One). As such, we welcome new terminology for a form of 'active nouns' which will move far beyond ordinary adjectives and will expedite our overall perception of a flowing and evolving world. (Hence, see the dog ruffling and snuffling in the anticipatory quiver of his new found self-awareness!) When we consider reality as energized and full of potential, we absorb the meaning of our own animated life within the pulse of an active universe. Keeping this in mind, will we keep the language as vibrant as reality; or, WILL THE (WORD!) REALLY GO TO THE DOGS?

STOP attempting to corner, capture, arrest and paralyze knowledge. It is far easier to lift yourself up by your own suspenders and carry yourself way up high, through the heavens, through space...

When we return to earth we look to science for hard facts and concrete evidence. However, the scientific community throws us off our feet (and down the hill) by fully accepting variables and inconsistencies within the vast majority of its own research experimentation. We add to this simple consideration the reality of scientists agreeing on two primary tenets: Nothing is absolute and Nature abhors a vacuum. Not surprisingly, these two statements have an extremely similar meaning. They both attest to the unpredictability of nature herself. Scientists can only keep their eyes wide open and only (momentarily) blink when their pens run out of ink. Hence, if the most 'straight' form of human analysis allows this much leeway in its perceptive understanding, clearly other schools of thought must accept huge contradictions in their own theoretical approaches. These factors of education and knowledge need to be considered when formulating hard opinions of our very own. When we close our eyes and mind to options and alternate points of view we deviate from the flexible, miraculous process of our own 'patented' human thought. In asserting an absolute conclusion we demonstrate the creativity of our own fiction and celebrate our own narrow escape from true reality. (Do we then become Intellectual Dumbos?...)

NEVER expect things to turn out a certain way unless you love disillusionment. In which case, ALWAYS expect things.

Reality is not solid. Therefore, absolute knowledge of tomorrow remains a mystery. We may in fact, utilize our memory to project a probable set of circumstances, which may occur in the very near future. However, formulating a direct expectation based upon this projected probability is extremely fallible. (Even witless, you might say.) Considering the multiplicity of factors involved in an interwoven reality, the mathematical possibilities brought together to create a future reality becomes exponentially astronomical. (Whipping out our long, slick calculators, we find it would take a hundred lifetimes to list even one-third of tomorrow's potential occurrences.) Naturally, it is far wiser to approach tomorrow with tenacity in our own ability to react to WHATEVER IT IS which the FUTURE holds in store for us. Besides, why spoil the effect of the huge bombshell which changes the rest of your life for the better (or for the worse?!!)

NEVER look a gift horse or any other horse, or any other large four-legged animal in the mouth. Be happy they accept your tiny two-legged self at all.

We share our world with a myriad of other life forms: professional wrestlers, cow tippers and televangelists to name but a few. Domestic animals, however, such as horses and dogs, which accept our presence and come to trust and befriend us, need to be esteemed, respected and rewarded. In no circumstance do we possess the right to mistreat or enslave these animals. In light of this elemental logic, remember: when your plow horse is tired, it deserves a long rest, and when your camel is thirsty, LET IT LEAD YOU to the oasis (or the kitchen sink or whatever...) There is no valid reason to sacrifice an animal's well being simply to satisfy your (and all of our own) human desires. We human beings create our own reality and therefore must suffer our own consequences. We hope evolution will eventually teach man to become the guardians of nature instead of her malevolent and pointless destroyer. (Otherwise, horses just may start acting like their not too distant cousins, the llamas, and spit masticated oats right into your vulnerable and altogether unsuspecting face. Eyes, nose, mouth, everything...) No horsing around this particular step!

FORGET all metaphors, cliches and parables.

This step is not to be taken literally. It is, however, a commentary about our misunderstanding of symbolism. All too often we mistake symbolic representation for actual literal truth. (Hell yes, we really do...) This is especially apparent in orthodox theology which formulates faith around exact passages and phrases found in antediluvian Holy texts. Whether or not these books are divinely inspired, their authors all utilized symbolism to demonstrate physical parallels (found in life) to their specific philosophical messages. Furthermore, because the word of God has always been beyond the full comprehension of man, prophets have always been asked (by God?) to translate the tenets of their faith and personal transfiguration in a commonplace and readily understandable manner. Naturally, through this human filtration system, religious texts became varied in their cultural language, terminology and national preconceptions. Where does all this WAYWARD history leave us? (Pretty much nowhere near any Holy lands I can think of...) As readers, we can only attempt to use symbolism to clarify all possible meanings beyond their colloquial and all too literal, transcripts. The only acceptable conclusion of all this commentary is this: God's ways may not be as strange as they seem, once you come to understand 'HIS' peculiar and particular lingo (instead of your own!...)

10

INVENT a paradoxical riddle and live with it the rest of your days, like: 'EVEN NOTHING IS SOMETHING...'

In order to break the mold of our preconceived ideologies, we need to practice new forms of contemplation. Accordingly, in our analysis of certain realities, we need to examine the apparent contradictions found within those realities. (Yeah, right!) One way to comprehend this type of thought process can be found in the visualization of a two-sided coin. Only one side of the coin can be seen at any one given time, nevertheless, the two-sided materiality of the coin is always completely understood: a buffalo on one side and a severed head on the other. In this sense, reality is neither this nor that, and contains a variety of conflicting meanings. Every aspect of the material world accommodates a multi-faceted, paradoxical and wholly complex set of possibilities within its physical design. So we see how truth challenges logic by remaining (simultaneously!) as elusive as a moth AND as stable as the ground beneath your feet. Speaking conservatively, TRUTH is a flip of a coin and a hard roll of the dice; at the same time, (that's right, simultaneously again!) truth may be a five year program with hard rollers at Bellevue Psychiatric, who took this seemingly harmless randomness of physics JUST A BIT TOO FAR...

11

BECOME a member of every religion on earth, including existentialism.

In order to understand our fellow human beings we must make an attempt to internalize the emotional significance of their communal system of faith and rituals. In this sense, existentialism is also a religion (or, system of faith.) It entails an elaborate belief in nature and the material universe. Its churches are located in the research library, national park and the corner coffee shop. Its monks wear little round glasses and carry overstuffed briefcases. In any case, we need to absorb the 'supposed' poignancy of every individual's personal faith. When we converse, commiserate and pray with our neighbors, we understand their complex fears of today and luminous hopes for tomorrow. We advance our own humanity when we break bread with our friends and neighbors and accept the validity of their belief system, whether it be in the parish, temple, open field or 'Frappe' shop. However, keep this in mind: the wise man seeks to understand realities questions, but never expects to fully possess her answers. (Reality, being at least half female, deserves at least 50% of her mystery, magic and above all, discretion...)

12

INVENT your own religion and make everyone on earth an automatic member.

The conceptualization of spiritual faith in a Supreme Being is an extremely personal matter. Therefore, when we accept the folds of humanity into our own private moral struggle we verify the equality of our fellow man. (Unless they try to pull into OUR parking space, the lowlife degenerates.) Rituals and methods of worship need not be specific and subsequently separatist. In this sense, simply by enacting our relative existence and real day to day manipulations, man theoretically embodies a form of rational (and logical) worship in God. Removing politics from religious faith enables a better understanding of its universal tenets. For example, all holy texts express God's love for His children. (Incidently, that would be us...) Realizing that the whole of humanity are the children of God (even the bozos who steal parking spaces,) we have the absolute right to unite all of these people into a loose congregation, (who worship by right of existence,) the one (#1) Supreme Being. Each time they take a breath of air, they would unconsciously do it because of this (#1) Supreme Being; call Him Nature, Godhead, Zeus, Jesus, Krishna, The Grateful Dead, whoever... In turn, this He/She/Source would silently bless the whole of the human race, every single one of us. (And yes, that would include the inane and witless motorists among us who nonetheless belong in wet, subterranean prison cells...)

13

TELL people who say, "knock on wood." to stop knocking on wood. Leave wood alone.

We must respect the life-span and magnificence of trees. This is not simply about shade. These living beings provide oxygen, food and shelter for multitudinous forms of wildlife. The detrimental environmental effects of deforestation is well documented in virtually all ecological studies. To simplify the dramatic conclusions of these studies we can confidently state that a world without trees would soon become a world void of all human life. (I know that thought pleases some of you, but unless you're an aardvark, humanity includes you.) This type of genocide is in no way an exceptionally intelligent way of life. The rainforest alone provides some two-thirds of the earth's overall oxygen supply. Accordingly, we need to find ALL of the alternative construction materials which fundamentally can replace wood. (Sorry all you nasal-throated environmental folk singers who play your cedar, maple and oak acoustic guitars.) More importantly, we absolutely can't afford to lose nature's precious RAINFOREST wood. Don't buy it. Don't sell it. Don't even think about it! In addition to saving existing forests, we need to plant more trees (and shrubs too, I'm afraid...) I'm proud to say, today, many states and townships across the globe express written laws enacting minimal tree planting requirements per each and every acre of already developed land. (Am I hallucinating, or has someone unleashed some branch of Intelligent Government, behind my sleeping back?)

14

ALWAYS talk to strangers. You already know the people you know.

In order to evolve as a society we need to recognize our fellow man. In a very real sense, no human being is a stranger to the human condition. Each and every one of us suffers the countless trials and tribulations encountered in this complex process of human life. (Your pet goldfish will never understand that. Of course, he has some real problems of his own...) In short, when we accept strangers into our personal existence, we acknowledge the rational brotherhood of all mankind. Furthermore, the psychological wall which we create in order to avoid contact with the fearful unknown effectively disintegrates as we reach out to persons new to our experience. Now then, WHAT WILL WE LEARN from overcoming this age-old barrier? We can haphazardly make three guesses: sometimes precious little, other times nothing at all, and still other times, far less than we actually expected. No doubt, it's one hell of a fundamental gamble. Notwithstanding, will we allow our petty fear of uncertainty hold us back from growing and adapting as a populace? Isn't that our goldfish's plan? (One more thing: please buy full-sized fish tanks for your pet goldfish, those 'traditional' goldfish bowls are just too dang small. It's worse than solitary confinement. It must be a cruel incarceration in there!)

NEVER buy things you need unless you're absolutely sure you NEED them.

In this statement we examine the detrimental effects of a wasteful society. The average United States consumer is consumed with an outright desire to buy himself status, position and ultimately material happiness. This mind-boggling consuming mania creates tons and tons of waste which steadily pollutes the planet and places us all into an uncertain ecological future (which basically blows!) Logically, self-worth will never be measured by a RUNNING COUNT of one's accumulated goods. (Just who wants to clean and maintain all this junk anyway?!) Instead, we are (and will always be) judged by our actions, deeds and consistency of character. When we finally decide only to purchase goods which we absolutely need, we will cut back tons of unnecessary global waste. This singular thoughtful deed will demonstrate our altruistic character and overall appreciation of nature and human life. Finally, today's consumer drive for high status will only deliver you into systematic economic slavery, while level-headed purchasing will ease your bills, stress and even adds dollars to you and your children's future. (No wonder Jesus never drove a B.M.W.)

16

STOP worrying about Alien Life Forms. They may need to be anonymous.

Alien species may or may not have mastered space travel and visited our own planet earth. (Quite frankly, I don't know.) But I do know one thing; if these life forms have the technology to create barely detectable space craft which visit our planet rather often, they certainly don't need our meddling help in their plans. Perhaps, they're studying human beings as our own scientists study common forms of bacteria. Perhaps some earthly knowledge will save their own plagued species from extinction. We can only speculate and watch as many 'B' movies as we possibly can. In any case, until aliens declare war on our very own planet we shouldn't lose too much sleep over the whole UFO question. Besides, have you noticed lately that faith in Aliens has replaced faith in God for a large number of sane individuals? My guess is Alien Cultures, like God, may only help those WHO HELP THEMSELVES...

EVERY day, once a day, think about the action of your breathing and slow it down. You'll find this deliberate breathing is a close cousin to meditation and will relax your central nervous system.

The human body is a highly complex mechanism. Nevertheless, it requires a stable outside environment of oxygen, water, protein and a multitude of other nutrients including, of course, vitamins and minerals. Once these environmental elements enter the human organism they effect all internal biological systems to create a 'stasis'. Stasis refers to an equilibrium of resonant energy which stabilizes the chemical exchange within the body. Internal organs utilize or 'burn' elements as they are required by an active body. When the body is involved in extreme movement, a larger amount of oxygen is required. Conversely, when the body is in a relaxed state, less oxygen is necessary. Slow, steady breathing provides a low stress 'stasis' for the entire physical structure. Meditation involves increasing the rate of breathing while remaining in a physically relaxed state. In this condition the body's residual energy slowly surges and creates a high stasis or internal 'burn' which aids the body's immune system and releases endorphins from the brain. This in turn produces a subtle euphoria which assists in entering the field of unconscious awareness. However, never rush the meditative breathing until you pass out. It is the rare wise man who is found by friends and family KNOCKED OUT COLD...

18

NEVER try to spit and sniff at the same time.

I tried this once and nearly swallowed my own tongue. Therefore, I wouldn't recommend it with any sincerity. However, if you find yourself blessed with this particular Coney Island-like sideshow skill, you may want to create an act and take it out on the road. Having mastered this unusual endeavor and having parleyed it into a multimillion dollar tour-de-force, you have the full right to tell all your friends to ignore this step! (With any luck, THEY won't swallow their own tongues.)

WHEN you're sitting around doing 'nothing', think about 'nothing', you may enjoy it more.

As the culmination of the most elaborate cognitive processes occurring in the human brain, 'Perception' and 'Awareness' have become the key components to our unique success as a species. (Although hot tubs, swedish massages and indoor plumbing aren't BAD innovations either.) Human beings are able to perceive an outside world of infinite complexity. At the same time we human beings can IMAGINE ourselves MANIPULATING and ACTING within that same reality. We have moved far beyond instinct and are now able to picture [or imagine] ourselves in the variable frame of temporal existence. (Let's see a salamander do THAT!) An awareness of 'nothing' clarifies and classifies its own beneficial psychological purpose. The contemplation of 'nothing', as practiced in traditional Yoga, frees the clutter of unnecessary information storage. For example: each day the advertizing machine seeks to program our neural hard drives with intense images of slick new things to buy. These bright new things are supposed to make our dull, drab lives colorful and complete. (BABOOM!!) The simple contemplation of 'nothing' erases these commercials and infomercials freeing valuable data space for the comprehension of the actual miraculous reality (which is in fact not new, but on summer days CAN BE too dang bright...)

20

ALWAYS enjoy yourself, even if it hurts.

Fundamentally, there is nothing wrong with the American work ethic; it teaches discipline, character and responsibility. However, unlike our European and Asian counterparts, and because of our work ethic, Americans place less emphasis on weekends, vacations and leisure time in general. Employers in the United States create few, if any, options for stress relief in the work place. Examples of these would include gymnasiums, game rooms and (my sweet lord!) swimming pools! Across the United States vacation time runs from two to three weeks, whereas our European comrades (NATO and all that...), enjoy six to eight week excursions from their particular modes of employment! Due to our relative SHORTAGE of fun, we Americans need to actively apply ourselves AND OUR NEIGHBORS in the real live pursuit of pleasure. We may quickly find that a good, hedonistic time begins simply by turning off the television set and greeting the great outdoors (hell, the porch will do.) But quite often, we'll just find ourselves too lazy (or just too tired) to go out and find adventure; instead we'll throw off our shoes and flick on the old t.v., radio or computer. Hell, if that's our idea of fun—THEN THAT'S EXACTLY WHAT WE SHOULD DO, in fact, we should keep doing that until it snaps our soft skull clean off our hard spinal cord! (Because we're Americans and it's still a free country! And that's just the way we like it.)

21

DO not live life waiting for the fulfillment of the future if the present is eating you alive.

ALL OUR LIVES We have been taught to 'save up for a rainy day' and to 'plan today for tomorrow'. This IS IN FACT sound and logical advice. However, the concept of today's sacrifice for tomorrow's reward simply doesn't hold water when today's sacrifice involves the eradication of our entire physical vitality and overall 'well- being'. Our actions in the present effect our health, character and sanity. Without these humanistic buttresses to support us, our appearance in the future may be as two-dimensional as the tombstone smugly resting above our dried-out heads. Consequently, if we dance, spin, swerve, fake and elude some of the more inane conservative conventions of today, we may just find ourselves high-stepping across the endzone of tomorrow. Besides, morticians hate bending all those real FROWNS into artificial SMILES. When it's time to go, greet the reaper with a happy face knowing full well you sacrificed when you had to, but at the same time you lived a full life too! Oh yeah, one for the books friend...

ON CHILDREN: Ask children questions, many questions, but never pass judgements on their answers.

Child psychologists and neurological researchers have recently come to a rather startling conclusion. Their findings dictate that the personality and behavior of an average human being is entirely formulated by the age of three. This means a child, two years prior to preschool, has already formulated an opinion about his actions in society and the absolute outside world. As parents, we can gain an insight into our children's attitudes and general perceptions simply by observing their interactive behavior; in other words, what allures them, and conversely, what repels them. As they get older we should be encouraged to ask them a variety of questions specifically concerning this set of behavior. Keep in mind, this is a learning process for the parent. Consequently, passing swift judgement on our children's responses may only serve to alienate them, and furthermore, turn their hard opinions inward in the form of repression. As the concerned parent listens to the child, he should ask the child to reason out all his gathered conclusions. In this process the child will begin to understand his prejudices and predispositions and begin to construct a parameter of self-awareness all by himself! The term 'education' literally means: to bring the knowledge out of'. Therefore, given time, the child will reveal himself to the outside world when he feels comfortable with the world which he perceives within himself. As the child overcomes his fears and gains confidence through the love and support of parents, he will eventually emerge like a veritable explosion upon the full playing field of life. At this point, give your baby sitter a huge raise and install her own phone line. It's for the best really...

ON CHILDREN: Buy toys that provide constructive creative ends. Buy games with objectives other than winning or losing.

The concept of winning and losing is a variation of the naturalistic behavior known as 'fight or flight' practiced by most living creatures. When faced with an enemy, an animal must choose to either hold its ground by fighting, or conversely, to preserve its life by fleeing to safety. Naturally, an incorrect choice may have dire consequences. Due to the significance of this event, animals train and practice with their siblings in order to gain as much strength, coordination and speed as possible. Eventually competitions ensue and the strongest, ablest pup emerges primed for his real status as group leader. However, human beings have developed rather new methods of hierarchy in this stage of evolution. This is why the 'nerd' is the boss and the 'jock' is the worker. We have over time created strategy, arbitration and social cohesion. In today's world, the winner represents the individual who is organized, creative and visionary as well as, strong, coordinated and fast (like the pup). Hence, our human games need to reflect our actual future needs. One day we may witness an olympic event called the 50 yard dash to virtual reality's time-space curve and return to the starting line as an older unit with zero forward tolerance and momentum. Stranger yet, we may one day be able to PARTICIPATE in olympic games from our very own comfortable living rooms. (Then will you be the ablest pup?)

ON CHILDREN: Explore with the child; do not teach your child, learn with your child...

Just because we're parents does not mean we possess the wisdom of the ages. Every time we step out of doors and perceive the living world around us, we find it new and unique, subtlety different in an astronomical number of ways. When we bring our children into the newness of this world, they witness it through eyes of wonder all their own. Consequently, we as parents, are able to learn as much from our children as they can learn from us. The trinity of Nature, God and the Unconscious are the true teachers, those archetypes represent respectively: matter, spirit and man's deepest awareness of both. As walking, talking adults we can reveal very little about the truth of existence. The child will learn the tenets of reality from his personal experiences in the outside world. In this world, the child will witness a bright and beautiful monarch butterfly suddenly captured in the web of a field spider who must sacrifice its victim's beauty solely in order to survive and maintain its own species. Accordingly, the child will learn the interplay of life and death: the complex and intricate methods of survival which bring about the goal of a secure, and sometimes sublime, existence. The combined effort of a gymnasium full of teachers, and (what the hell) an assistant vice-principle thrown in for good measure, still cannot guarantee the same results of wisdom taught to a child by two simple bugs in a field...

STOP relying on the forebrain. The forebrain is a special piece of equipment. Our over-dependent use of it, the dominance of it within our brain, is completely antiquated.

The logic which we assemble in our waking consciousness is indeed formidable. Our forebrain and opposable thumb has taken us ever higher up the mountain called civilization. In fact, each passing year, our logic and methodology creates finer and more precise tools for latching onto and climbing the immeasurable heights of civilization. Yes sir, we are headed up the mountain and no force on earth can bring us down. But why do we feel this urge to climb at all? What is atop the mountain? Why must we get higher than we were before? Logic can only speak about the concrete and the so-called factual. Therefore, logic is unable to tackle the question of man's spiritual desire, his inspiration and his genius. We can postulate that MAN is an evolving creature, yet we cannot formulate specifics as to why MAN happens to be that way in the first place. The forebrain calculates, compares and focuses best possible results. However, the reptilian brain carries instinct and reactive behaviorism which the forebrain absolutely requires to remain intact. We must take both aspects into account and every developing aspect in between. In truth, the deepest awareness of our Unconscious mind is the 'spirit', or 'total package', of all aspects of our neurological physiology. This is why the scientist cannot replace the visionary and vice-versa. Along these same lines, the well-tested occult practices of the East cannot be at odds with the scientific methodology of the West (and again, vice-versa.) If we are to be whole, we must embrace the union of all our worldly experience and collected wisdom. (I mean, can't we all just get along?)

NEVER concentrate too hard on finding an answer. Eventually, like any other stroke of genius, a valid answer will find its way into your brain if you clarify exactly what the question or problem may be. In many cases, answers are hidden within the context of the questions themselves.

All questions presuppose an answer. In most cases, we accept the best, or most appropriate, answer. Mathematics demonstrates the process behind this particular assimilation of logic. In working our way toward a coherent determination, we break down the mathematical question, or problem, into its finite set of realities. When we apply the rules of calculation upon the numerals in these subsets they provide ever simpler and more precise numerals. When we are left with the simplest set of numerals, we calculate their ultimate relation. Having accomplished this feat, we are able to provide an answer which applies to the original mathematical question. In this methodology we have witnessed the scientific method at work: breaking down a physical whole into its discriminate parts and analyzing the precise relations of these parts in order to understand the unification of all processes. Now, (that is, if we still could care less) we can answer any given question, having broken it down to its simplest parts, and determining the exact point by point objective of its rational inquiry. In this sense, we should always answer a question with a question. Some annoying people (like myself) answer certain questions with as many as seven entirely unrelated questions in order to probe the real source of a powerful inquisition. (Unfortunately, this is also why I find myself eating alone in otherwise crowded restaurants.)

DON'T feel sorry for things. Help or don't help, and shut up about it.

We all face the reality of wasted time. As we concern ourselves with the political back and forth bickering of what needs to be done in a difficult social situation, the dire situation continues to occur. People are living on the streets, hungry and destitute. Each day we question why we feel so horrible, so moody and so lackluster in our own every day lives; meanwhile, outside our very doors their exist people who are cold, hungry and trying to raise children in outright squalor. These people are in need of help RIGHT NOW. We must move beyond our petty concerns and assimilate the reality of human suffering. If we wish to decrease the misery of the world, we have an absolute prerogative to act upon our concerns and assist the poor and needy HOWEVER we can. (Let's deviate for a moment shall we?) Many famous individuals have taken their own lives because they were unable to handle the fast-paced price of their own fame: John Belushi, Jim Morrison, Kurt Cobain, Janis Joplin, the list goes on and on. I appeal to all you wealthy individuals who have given up on life. Give some of your fortune to those who want to live: who want a second chance at life. Life is precious and life is the sum total of all things. Those who do not agree with the previous statement should (at least in some tangible way) make a path for others. Give up on reality, on life, and you give up on social sympathy. Choose life and you give life to someone who appreciates its real worth and meaning. We are given just one good life; we should do what we can to provide a worthwhile existence for those a little less fortunate than ourselves. (O.K. lectures over, now we can go make sure our vaults are still safe, solid and secure!)

SOME ideas are incomprehensible for some people, so never let what people say about your ideas dive too deeply into your brain.

There seems to be an accepted language in the society of man which dictates right and wrong, correct and incorrect. We seem to be possessed by an unarticulated set of human rules WHICH MUST BE, NONETHELESS, ADHERED TO. If we do not follow these rules we risk being chastised by the majority of our peers. How these rules, or norms, come into being is an absolute mystery, nevertheless, they place an unbelievable strain on individuals who wish to deviate from anticipated roles and wish to create their own realties. Every day we fight for our freedom and our true Americanism. In a real sense, we really need not respond to this infantile peer pressure at all. As actual proof of this, note the ultra-hip in American society reject ALL choices of 'hip' or 'politically correct' behavior followed by the recognized masses. This means if you are unique and alienated, you are among the elite and cosmopolitan hipsters of this world. I fully agree it's really not a big deal, but it does have its rationalizing comfort. If a champagne drinking billionaire bravado from SoHo thinks its alright to wear only green while avoiding sunlight, how bad can it be? He seems to have a better handle on life than the your local ex-prom queen who may unfortunately face a 'normal', yet stormy, life of repeated suffering and disillusionment. (What do you think?...)

DRINKING booze or beer is not the key to great sex.

Admittedly, alcohol may erase certain fears and apprehensions while increasing hormonal levels produced by adrenal glands. However, alcohol is also a depressant and a retardant, which means it slows down all of your body's physiological processes. This means your mind may want to do it, but your body (in full defiance) may just want to kick back and enjoy the sunset and gentle breeze. In this situation there is nothing the would-be lover can do except to wait until the effects of his personal alcohol intake wear off. Naturally, this is not the most romantic (or virile) of situations. James Bond and Matt Helm (two modern, mythical heroes) drank socially to demonstrate the ease of their cinematic spying existence. This is quite different than the ordinary individual who drinks until his own hands seem unrecognizable and suspect of treason. We need to limit our intake of alcohol in the process of achieving our paramount sexual climax. It is one thing to be utterly beside ourselves with euphoria and quite another to be on the floor writhing in the all-too-human misery of gastronomical discharge. Forget the boozed-up crooners, the spirit of the age has changed, now nimble and fully functional types, seem to be most actively desired by would-be mates. (Sorry Frankie...)

30

COFFEE and jacuzzis are the key to great sex.

Sex is energetic and spirited. It is hungry and primal. We move toward the opposite sex with an almost reckless abandonment which demonstrates our natural and God-given ability to continue the species with vigor and confidence. I learned this in a movie theater when I was fifteen. (Actually, I saw it happening up there on the big, bright screen. I was alone at the time.) In any case, the myth of sexuality, the fantasy of it, was revealed to me. I witnessed why sex involved tension, struggle, and then release. I learned the power of sexuality was born from its 'stimulation'. Still today, the seductress and the tempter bring us to the edge. We grow nervous in the excitation of our hormonal reaction. We are tempted by the forbidden fruit and the ecstacy of losing ourselves. Yet, there is a flip side to this primal sexuality; it is known as 'the safety net'. It is often said that when we experience sex with someone we love we experience the best sex of all. This is a fair (if not redundant) statement. We feel secure (safe) with someone we love and we wouldn't 'love' them if we didn't 'desire' (that is, become stimulated) by them in the first place. Consequently, in this safe realm of unbridled passion it is quite natural for us to gleefully release our sense of worldly bounds and enter a rather ecstatic and paradise-like union. Coffee and jacuzzis represent this twin world of stimulation and a relaxed state of mind fully reminiscent of that gargantuan creature known as l'amour. (Not to be confused with marriage and prenuptial contracts which deliver quite another story entirely...)

NEVER do things that make you feel bad, unless, feeling bad makes you feel good.

The responsible side of our being is forever preoccupied with self-denial. We have been programmed to believe that 'good things' can come to us only as a result of our own personal suffering. In this sense, we have a sort of built-in martyrdom, patiently waiting to sacrifice itself (that is, ourselves) solely to assist others (friends, family, whoever...) in the course and cause of good. This altruism is noble, but in today's world, fairly unnecessary. We live in a time where people respect healthy individualism. We believe friendship should not be freely given, but rather, earned. Today's modern individual is drawn toward his self-sufficient counterpart, who depends on very little, and hence, commands trust and respect. We are instead repelled by persons who give up entirely too much of themselves, simply to be accepted. Human beings feel far more comfortable leaning on sturdy trees, rather than yielding branches. From another standpoint, there exists a cycle of co-dependance, wherein persons learn to rely on others (government, community etc.) for their own well being. This dependency causes (these) people to lose all sense of self-worth and the accompanying ability to achieve and succeed on their own. At a very early age a child takes his first brave steps into 'individuation' where he first dares to understand and exist in the living world on his own terms. When we challenge life in this way, we appreciate our own risks and as such, accept our own richly deserved rewards. Behind the call of freedom and American individualism lies the real pursuit of happiness. Marie Antoinette once said, "Let them eat cake!" (WELL, royalty is history!) And while democracy still rules, (albeit, working out its kinks,)

I say we all take that second helping of Marie's cake. If we are to be whole human beings, we must wholeheartedly relish this life, which could (and probably should) be our last...

32

FEELING good is not the same as being good.

Step thirty-two is the brake mechanism of step thirty-one. It expresses our need to differentiate our internal actions and their external consequences. Let us elaborate. As stated, freedom does allow and desire us to feel good. However, freedom is designed for everybody, universally. That means that if your particular freedom and pleasure imposes and blocks the freedom and pleasure of another, you have entirely forfeited its entire intention and significance. Freedom, in order to work, must be democratic and ABSOLUTELY cannot be selective. Old Marie Antoinette was very free in her time, but her pleasure came at the full expense and outright pain of most of her subjects and especially, her peasants. Consequently, they chopped off her head and played dust volleyball with its rather regal roundness. We are no different than old Marie, when we act as an isolated island all unto ourselves, losing all mortal concern and respect for everyone around us. In order for our own freedom to be preserved, we must preserve the freedom of others. It's that simple. Accordingly, when we enact our freedom, we may want to have a quick look around. We don't want to be torturing, sodomizing, murdering, or just generally offending anyone else. (I mean, can't we all just get along?)

IF you can feel good and be good at the same time, you're not half bad.

Attaining an equal amount of self-awareness and social awareness is a paramount accomplishment. It implies the ability to sense the subtle requirements of an outside world while creating a delicate balance of one's own specific needs. This combination of external and internal awareness indicates a high development of all five senses and the emotional and intellectual hardware needed to empower them. Choosing wisely for oneself, AND at the same time, satisfying the needs of others, as best we can, brings us as close to real tranquility (happiness baby!) as we can possibly hope for as human beings. However, we can't be unrealistic about this 'holistic' approach. Very often our own desires drastically clash with those of our peers in the outside world. After all, no two people are exactly alike. Accordingly, we must find a middle ground and compromise our interests. This often involves elaborate gives and takes, checks and balances. Unfortunately, and quite often, some people are prepared to take but are simply unable to give. In this confusing state of affairs, we must be able to give without expecting anything in return. At the same time, we must be cautious not to be taken advantage of in our good-hearted martyrdom. In short, we must juggle the ball of personal happiness, and quite frankly, this often takes the fun right out of it!

WHEN you're not half bad you're unbalanced; so work yourself up to being more or less exactly half-bad once again.

The universe is an interplay of positive and negative forces which curve space and create in the process a spiral continuum of material existence. From protein-filled DNA strands to opposable thumbs, elliptical moons and solar-driven polarized galaxies, reality expresses itself in what seems to be a favorable circular fashion. Considering paths of linear movement, we find the shortest route found in continuous back and forth motion is the 360 Degree curved pathway known as 'spin'. The electromagnetic/positive-negative force of this spin powers the muscle-driven pulse our own human organs and ultra-sensitive neuro-spinal systems. Our psychological behavior, consistent with this same electro-static brain wave activity, fluctuates from elation to aggression, depression, fear and every coordinate in-between. In this elaboration, it is unrealistic and fundamentally unnatural for a human being to display one-sided, one-dimensional emotional and overall psychological behavior. In the world of psychology, a well adapted individual is considered to be a well-balanced person who 'tempers' his behavior according to external stimuli. In other words, we learn when and where to use certain and exact compass coordinates of our 360 Degree variable of personality. This is why a person who laughs hysterically at funerals, train wrecks and burning buildings is considered to be a just a LITTLE BIT off-kilter...

ART is not static. The trick is not in the making, but rather in the unraveling.

Art is a very human and active two-way street of 'creation' and 'perception'. In the real-time combining enactment of mind, spirit and emotion, the artist releases the creative culmination of his entire being. Having accomplished this feat, he must then stand back and perceive the composition of relativistic elements which he has (unconsciously!) chosen to bring together. He will then fine tune his creation by bringing it ever closer to the perception of his original creative 'vision'. As OUTIDE VIEWERS appraising the completed art work, we (unconsciously!) reverse this entire dynamic process. As such, we perceive in the present moment of observation, the end result of the complete artistic process, replete with history, internal mood, motivational changes and fine incremental tuning. At this point, the creative work reconstructs itself in the elaboration of our own creative perception. In other words, we probe the depths of the artist's insight and ability and process it against our own dynamic principle. We are moved by the work because it reveals formidable, yet entirely real, levels of our own deepest (unconscious!) selves. The work outlines our own sensitive humanity and furthermore, our virtual human potential. The art work is a masterpiece because the perceiving human creature such as he or she is: is (him or herself) a genuine masterpiece of creation too. After all, it must take some level of divine wonder to truly appreciate any of Andy Warhol's movies...

IT will make you feel better if you know that all creation is the destruction of some other space. Whatever comes INTO being takes something else OUT of being.

Modern physics postulates that matter is neither created or destroyed. In other words, nothing new comes into existence; instead, matter changes its shape, form and atomic number in accordance to environmental necessity. Relative outside forces direct this morphing mechanism and the end result is 'stasis' or 'bodies at rest'. When we embody the hands and eyes of an artist, we choose at that moment to alter a pre-existing form of matter to reflect our own symbiology and impression of the world. We cover the virgin white canvas with our torrid enamels of experience and horror, we mold the clay into the vapid gargoyle of our darkest spirits undaunted and we place the music of the spheres into an organized rhythm of our own circular elation and reverberating cacophony. In short, man (in the mold of reality itself,) destroys the world, in order to create the world anew.

ON CHILDREN: If possible, instill within the child an appreciation and love for the variety and splendor of nature. Once again remember, children learn from observation, not from lecture.

There is a misconception began in the world of pre-antiquity, that man and nature are entirely separate entities locked in an eternal struggle against one another. Along the lines of this rather perverse ideology, the Holy Bible states that man has ultimate dominion over all the earth and all the creatures which inhabit it. In this sense, man is given divine permission to 'overcome' nature wherever possible, in order to fashion his own 'ideal' civilization. Of course, this mode of thinking came into existence in a time when men were routinely killed in storms, eaten by crocodiles and tigers, bitten by snakes and wolverines and poisoned by a thousand different and unique plants each and every day. Our overriding trepidation dictated our intelligence to clear out nature (most of it, anyway) and build tight little villages and towns, isolated and secure from nature's forbidding elements. Over the years we have come to terms with nature. We have even befriended it. Each and every day we use its essential gifts to enhance the quality of our lives on earth. Following the acumen of men like Charles Darwin, we learned how we ourselves rose up from nature's primal pools of protein in progressive steps. We human beings are yet another formidable chapter of nature herself and therefore our existence, regardless of how bizarre it may seem, is as natural as that of any shiny slug, sinewy grasshopper or slobbering wilderbeast...

ON CHILDREN: REMEMBER you are a role model. Be expressive and imaginative: experience the world with wonder: keep in mind, the child inside you never vanished.

Not too long ago, (in our great-great grandfather's day,) children were not regarded as children, but rather as miniature adults. Ironically, this seemingly ludicrous tenet may just hold true today, only in reverse! That is to say, adults are not adults, but rather gigantic children. If you consider the atomic bomb, acid rain, leather neckties, televangelists and the advertizing machine in corporate America operating in full swing, its not too difficult to understand the underlying premise of this seemingly obtuse statement. No harm done; we create our nefarious games as we deem them necessary. The point is we are all overgrown children. In this state of affairs, it is only natural for us to run, twist, jump and play with our own children. With trust grows confidence and with confidence grows independence. If we as adults can invent the hoola-hoop, the chia pet and the vegomatic all in the same century, just imagine what our children's young and fertile minds may come up with simply to astound and amaze US!

ON CHILDREN: IF possible, explain what you as an adult perform and accomplish every day, surprisingly enough, even mundane ADULT endeavors may be fascinating to your children.

Our adult world and our adult jobs are by and large fairly zany. As we keep the capitalistic ball rolling as best we can in order to satisfy our own needs, we seem to be expanding upon a puzzle of growing immensity and inflating preposterous ingenuity. In short, with each passing minute we seem to be rationalizing the very sanity of our own means of existence. As a direct cause and effect relationship, it justifiably may be our responsibility as human beings to let our children observe the game of our own (sane?) adulthood. As we churn out civilization, our children may pick up a thing or two about their own futures in life. We must be honest with ourselves; in most cases, children look up to us simply because they don't know any better. It would be foolish for us not to capitalize upon this lucky twist of generational fate to widen THEIR outlook on the world in general and in particular. Their young eyes can only expand upon and eventually clarify our own worldly wizardry and carnivalesque style of life here on earth. Our children represent our next evolutionary adaptation. If we're lucky, when our children's children come to fullest attainment and highest realizations, they won't throw us all in jail, or nasty, unpainted insane asylums...

STOP relying on a storehouse of information bits. Make connections, challenge conclusions and then, discover the amazing lattice-work of our miraculous intertwining reality.

Earlier in this text, we explored the scientific advantage of utilizing the primitive, instinctual centers of our brain. We now turn to the social tenets of this very same argument. In new relationships, potential mates often make the mistake (blunder actually!) of concentrating too hard upon their physical behavior and illuminated personality. In attempting to 'sell ourselves', we often lose sight of the innate, yet very real, feelings which are ever present in all social interactions. In attempting to transmit our own highest frequency, we forget to receive the transmissions of our counterparts in the overall real life connection. Emotions encountered in this socialization must be addressed, understood and (Yawn!) eventually worked out. Our gifts of language and intellectualism become (absurdly!) useless when they are removed from our hard-hitting emotionalism. To make matters worse, we sometimes bury ourselves deeper into trouble with mountains of supposedly reconstructive verbal refuse. (A bit of spiritual advice: shut up and give the friggin' thing a chance...)

CONSIDER eating more insects and fewer animals. I know it may seem repelling, but insects are protein-filled and plentiful, while animals are being systematically mistreated and locked away in great warehouses for the general feeding of mankind: which is absolutely repellent.

It's rather ironic that we enjoy eating living creatures who are anatomically similar to ourselves. As such, we prefer eating animals over fish, fish over reptiles, and further down the line, we prefer eating large, cold-blooded reptiles over insects. The more alien and unique the creature appears, the less appealing it becomes. In this sense, it's a wonder we aren't all cannibals. (Living in NYC, I sometimes wonder if we really aren't all cannibals, the way we bark and flash yellow teeth at one another.) In any case, environmentalists and natural scientists express a concern about the exponential expansion of insect-life upon the planet. Many of these professionals assure that insects will ultimately inherit the earth, becoming the next extraordinarily dominant form of species-life. Where this leaves humanity raises some rather horrifying questions... Considering all this, shouldn't we be asking our master chefs to reduce these plentiful, peculiar pests into simple, crunchy culinary treats? (If you can't beat em', eat em'!)

IF you're a vegetarian, consider eating more nuts and fewer stems and leaves. Remember, plants are living breathing life forms too.

A plant offers food in exchange for seed propagation. The rose really doesn't care if you think it's pretty or if your girlfriend thinks its sweetness symbolizes true romance. It only wants the outside world to be attracted to its pollen in order to continue its own species. Of course, there is nothing wrong within this master plan. To this end, we should only feed ourselves with the plant's freely offered vegetable, grain, fruit or nut, making certain that the seeds found within these offered food sources are in turn planted and generously harvested. In this perfect chain of subsistence and rebirth nothing is harmed, ravaged or wasted. We have moved far beyond the 'slash and burn' level our evolutionary development. Consequently, eat hearty, eat smart and in true post, post modern fashion become a punk rock Johnny Rotten Appleseed and (with your best british accent) go Johnny Rotten Appleseed go, go, go, GO!!!

43

NEVER eat plastic, metal or rubber.

There is a reason why we invented the word: edible. There are simply some meals we need to turn down. As a general rule of thumb, if the meal is harder, sharper and more durable than beef jerky, stay away from it. If the food is heat resistant, shock resistant and beads water, you may need to have a second look too. However, all man-made foods are not necessarily inedible. Some man-made foodstuffs, (while not nutritious in any real way,) may in fact be entirely edible. Some are even tasty in a kind of mind numbing sort of way. As far as Trace Elements go, see your doctor; some people may require light minerals, while others may find themselves perishing away without a good dose of heavy metal. Ozzy Osbourne himself is not entirely unaware of which foods are edible and which are not: (veggies: Always, bats: Never)

IF possible, enjoy defecating, it's a great celebration.

Whenever we 'release' anything, there is a determination made to relieve pressure and give up on the tension of a struggle. In short, when we defecate, we allow our bodies to come to rest. Moreover, when we throw off the excess of all our material byproducts, we are in a very real sense, purifying our entire physiological structure (translation: our bodies!) This release and purification leads to general good health, good sensations and overall well being. So by all means, sit down and enjoy yourself!

45

MAKE every bodily function a great celebration, not just sex.

The correct functioning of the human body sings in a circular, living symphony of movement, interplay, charge, resonance and ultimately, transfiguration. This animated dance of pure reason is etched upon the very building blocks of our collaborative DNA blueprint. However, the enactment of this choreography depends in part on our experiential awareness of self. When our minds are in tune with our bodies, (as in the tantric arts of yoga, tai-chi and karmic circular prayer,) we lift the animated spirit of our physical being to the satori threshold of pure soul, what we call the universal soul. (Now that's heavy!) However, we need to remember that AWARENESS of the smallest function of our body is equally as important as the AWARENESS of the entire body itself. Ultimately, no single spark of life is taken for granted. As such, each time our heart beats its miraculous pulse of life we return to proclaim the infinite scope of existence in greater detail and with more profound appreciation than ever before. (But that's only if you get INTO that sort of thing. You know?...)

46

WEAR comfortable clothes, regardless of whether they're tight or loose. Remember, clothes are your skin. They are wrapped up in your psyche.

We each have our own peculiar tastes about what clothes may or may not look fashionable upon us. No harm done. There's enough room in the world for every imaginable style. However, THERE IS ONE consideration in the very best choice of our own daily apparel. The clothes we wear should roughly conform to the general shapes of our bodies. When clothes do not conform to our form, we run the risk of having (various!) materials dig into our fleash and hamper our cardio-vascular circulation. Moreover, when proper heat and toxin ventilation is blocked (or utterly denied,) the bodily immune system becomes under siege! This consistent interruption can lead to a whole slew of infections and disease. Of course, no rule is etched in stone and freedom is paramount to our daily humanity. Consequently, if you must wear those paint-on pants, form-hugging beach wear, or S&M battle regalia, at very least remember to remove them when you sleep at night. (Regardless of your planned morning activities of high-impact degradation...)

SING as often as you can, even, if you sing like a dying water bison.

Notwithstanding the immortal blues and the mesmerizingly tragic swan song, singing is not often associated with depression. When we belt out the warbling melody which illuminates our diaphragm, chest, throat and finally mouth, we courageously project ourselves into the big, wide world. Our song confirms our animated confidence in self. We welcome the whole world to notice our singular and utterly unique existence. Moreover, the circular breathing involved in the art of singing can be a rhythmic meditation releasing pleasure-giving endorphins into our cerebro-spinal chemical ladder. In fact, this externalization of self expands the resonant energy of our entire physical being. In an instant, we transmit a swelling source which pulses from within our infrastructure out to the receiving and absolute spectral prism of our extraordinary environment. We sing the song of angels, devils and fairie folk of every size, shape and demeanor. We release ghost-like, the heart of the age in which we live, and in so doing, we challenge time to erase the mark which we presume to leave behind to future generations. (Whether they want it or not.)

DON'T be afraid to touch people, it helps confirm their true reality.

We live in a world where we are saturated by live, technicolor images. Individuals thrown into the glare of the media become 'larger than life', unreachable and almost spirit-like (both angels and devils.) We tend to worship these persons who are unreachable and seem so unlike ourselves. Naturally, or rather unnaturally, the media is purposely crafted to continuously create these illusions; our story-telling human characterizations continue to be bent on keeping heroes and myths alive. Unfortunately, this curse of the media, namely creating living myths to generate entertainment values, causes these living myths, or STARS, to go underground, hiding from the very public which enables their rather strange 'stardom' in the first place. Adoring fans want to touch and experience the physical truth of their heroes and myths, so much so, that STARS (who are NOT mythical persons) fear being ripped limb from limb by mobs of admirers. Naturally, celebrities are highly mortal and highly fallible, and sadly, their real, down-to-earth humanness is taken away from them in their new-found technicolor status of heroic symbolism (sorry lads.) Fortunately, we're NOT ALL STARS and as such, we can reach out and touch our friends, family, peers and even strangers, (who we can welcome with firm clasps into the circle of our eccentric entourages!)

THERE are many people in this world who enjoy BE-
ING HURT, who LOVE PAIN; THEY are the people you
should hurt IF you need to hurt someone. They may even
pay you for it! However, don't get too carried away. Remember, there are ninety-nine other steps in this book...

Marquis de Sade might have said, "There are only two
kinds of people in this world: sadists and masochists!" A
century later, naturalist Charles Darwin might have said,
"There are only two kinds of animals in this world: predators and prey." Both statements would be at least partially
correct. For REASON, not entirely understood, life has always manifested VICTIMS and VICTIMIZERS. Even today, psychologists speak about Type A (aggressive) and Type
B (passive) personalities. We fathom in this (either-or) dis-
cussion a naturalistic balance which seems to exist solely
to counter-balance life itself. As such, we allow the dominants to seek out the submissives and vice-versa. We in-
nately understand when dominants are paired off together
and submissives are paired off together, arguments, fighting and eventually world wars develop AND SUCCEED.
Why waste our personalities on these useless struggles?
Find your BEST counterpart!

NEVER take what anybody says too seriously, but listen to everything.

Only you can truly know yourself. This being the case, ANY AND ALL advice given to you should be scrutinized and weighed against your own experience and sensibility. On the other hand, humans share a common evolutionary history. As such, each human being is intimately related to all his brothers and sisters in the REAL species pool. This is why virtually everyone you meet can (and most likely will!) teach you something new about the human experience. Thus, we need to (at very least!) listen to advice given, WITHOUT becoming brainwashed by the tasty tidbits of readily offered wisdom. At this point, I MUST take exception to fanatical biblical rhetoric. No rule or truth is written in stone and every reality has a complex gray area surrounding its ultimate meaning. Accordingly, we must utilize our gifts of reason, instinct and passion in the slow and careful deliberation of all behavioral suggestions AND proposals. (Including this one!...)

PURCHASE a durable notebook and write down all your good ideas. It's shameful how many good ideas we all forget.

Not taking anything away from memory, the written word has advanced us more as a species than all other external neurological adaptations combined. The expansive resource of chronological textbooks elucidating an ongoing process of education delineated throughout human history steers us into future consciousness with focus, accuracy and above all: confidence. (Yawn!) Each of us PARTICIPATES in this modern culmination of conscious human awareness. Consequently, all our thoughts and conceptualizations add to the overall scope of human knowledge. (To a greater or lesser degree, naturally.) The miracle of life demonstrates the precise correlation between the macrocosm and microcosm. In other words, the tenets which hold true for the universe, also hold true for the individual. Hence, our personal ideas accurately construct the complex psychological perspective of a very real and otherwise entirely objective reality. Furthermore, when we write the journal of our experience, we unlock the resource of our greatest potential and (blah...blah...blah...blah...) You get the idea.

DON'T be afraid to scream from time to time. I like to go up to the roof when I scream. Most of the time, it's better to scream around midday, for your neighbor's sake.

Our body is a complex electro-chemical battery which stores and releases energy according to its appropriate physiological needs. Unfortunately, our modern society often necessitates us to concentrate high levels of stress-absorbing energy without allowing a balanced release of the very same neuro-chemical force. In lieu of this precarious situation, we need to find alternate ways to redistribute our nervous impulses (without using a machete.) A good sound scream will often release physical pressure from both the body and the mind. Other healthy forms of release include: punching bags, high-impact aerobics, marathon dancing and for those of us over 47, several forms of consensual copulation...

IT is healthy to get your frustrations out, but if you find yourself frustrated all too often, it may mean you need to change some very real and crucial aspects of your life.

Our unconscious reveals changes which are necessary in our life via recurring dreams. All too often, we find ourselves caught up in the perilous machinations of our social and economic existence. Our dreams reflect this torturous reality which engulfs our freedom and attacks our sanctity. Nevertheless, we become frozen in terror at the thought of the large upheavals which may be necessary in our every day lives in order to negate these problems. Consequently, we accept our suffering rather than taking on undoubtedly required risks. This unchallenging behavior is fine for hermit crabs, garden snakes and tree slugs. Human beings, on the other hand, possess the ability to reason and deliberate upon appropriate choices. Society, evolution and the evolution of society, has given us a relative amount of freedom of choice. Sometimes our long-term security depends on our courage to venture into terrifying terrain when it is initially deemed necessary. Nothing is guaranteed in life, but life becomes certain death without movement, change and the subsequent newness of ALL THIS EXPERIENCE. 'Just do it' was a reality, long before it was a slogan for expensive sneakers...

DON'T be afraid of change. Bumpy roads lead to high places too.

It is said that character builds destiny. This simple phrase rings true because it is born from a social structure which honors and respects powerful character. There exists an often repeated written tradition throughout our living history which quotes that the personality which defines genuine character is chiseled and molded ever finer and stronger by the harsh blows of a difficult existence. Today, as before in the most ancient of times, truth is revealed by overcoming our own hardships. As we wholly embody their realistic threats and tragedies and become ever grander and deeper in our empathy, knowledge and spirit. If we are not THROWN ASUNDER by life's obstacles, we soar ever higher to our own intangible capacity. Ancient sculptures, such as Michelangelo's David, define this immortality of the human spirit. We notice why the objective symbolism is extremely relevant in ancient art such as Michelangelo's David, as it demonstrates the frailty of our human forms of clay. Clay which (in the presence of great faith) may be shaped by reason, emotion and soulful vision into refined reflections of (God's?) miraculous reality. Without all this, CHARACTER WILL SIMPLY DRIP DESTINY down the sewers of St. Marks Place, unnoticed even by the squatters...

DON'T be afraid of high places; we need more humble people who are honestly cautious of lofty rank governing in the agency of these distinguished capacities.

How many politicians demonstrate flashy insincerity and pompous self-inflatement? Have you lost count? The truth is the day of the humble leader is still awaiting. Government is complex, multi-layered and multi-dimensional. Therefore, elected officials owe their constituents a well-run, hard working team of experts who take their jobs seriously and place policy making far ahead of megalomania and political jockeying. A simple, dedicated group of men and women who are willing to take the time to measure diverse political arguments and structure reasonable compromises which push society in a positive and progressive direction is, for some unknown reason, not so easy to find. We may in fact need to change the mind-set of our young, and up and coming, politicians. "We the People" still begins our democratic treatise and whole American philosophy. Our forefathers wanted simple people to run government, not power hungry kings, lords and emperors. We live in a land forged by the hot passion of these liberated ideas. For this reason alone, we cannot slip back into an undemocratic and entirely primitive style of leadership. (We should erase the irresponsible and unnecessary cult of personality, before it erases us...)

IF you're a 'know it all', call your local government and let them know about it 'all'. If they're not interested, call me. I've always been a firm believer that you can never know too much.

We live in the information age. However, we need to remember this successful technical advancement in history did not occur overnight. Years of research, experimentation and painstaking stages of development elevated our species into the hypersensitive age of the radar, satellite and microchip. We are linked today as a global community more than ever before in human history (yikes!). This means a shopkeeper from Hong Kong can casually converse with a yippy from Seattle who is partners with a Pakastani coffee-bean grower who is best friends with a Hawaiian surfer living from wave to wave on the internet sea. In such a global environment, information is paramount and wholly expected from each and every one of us. The implication of this line of thought reveals that in today's world nothing which seems pertinent to oneself should be kept to oneself (uh oh!). Today, opinions, theories and beliefs alike enjoy a high-tech platform and immense multi-cultural audience. This healthy discourse of our collected knowledge, diverse interests and faiths can only further the ultimate parameters of our future-bound humankind. (!)

BUY many clocks and set them all for different times. You may be late, you may be early, but you'll always be on time.

This may be a rat race, but we are not rats. The measurement of time was created to enhance our perception of the environment in order to coordinate our rituals in accordance to the daily temporal allotment. In other words, time was created for our absolute convenience. Logic tells us in no way was time developed for our ultimate enslavement. Yet, good plans, every now and then, have a way of becoming horribly twisted and distorted into some gruesome polarity of what they once stood for. Time today, like some Roman guard, cracks a whip and pounds a mindless, hypnotic drum. Enough is enough already. In the most simplest of terms, general etiquette and human kindness motivate us to be on time (or roughly thereabouts) to meet (or relieve) one another (in the workplace or some other place.) Moreover, once in the workplace, the idea of toiling as much labor out of a person in an eight-hour period as humanly possible is utterly absurd. Our economic system has no right enslaving our basic humanity. Some people are naturally slow, others fast. We are not robots and we are not rats. History and technology has demonstrated the relative ease of a well thought-out existence. Money hungry corporate barons cannot deny us our own modern reality. Life should be easier today than it was two-hundred or two-thousand years ago. After all, slavery was abolished. Right?

IF you're a shy person, don't be afraid to fantasize about being outgoing. Fantasy can be the best reality and many times role-play leads to the actual performance.

Imagination and visualization are key components in the enactment of physical reality. We instantaneously place ourselves into the rough parameters of new realities with each and every passing moment of our lives. Zen mystics and high-level marshall artists who 'react precisely in the living moment' have practiced and honed this mastery utilizing years of creative visualization as their ideal, yet working, guide. This means their mental projection and physical reality are close enough to reveal one single action which appears nearly miraculous to the common observer. This text has repeatedly stressed the importance of creating oneself both inside and out. To this end, we need to clearly paraphrase all our internal objectives, goals and desires. Consequently, before we externally create ourselves, we will have determined our most lasting and fulfilling purpose in this particular life. With reason, sanity and faith, we can progressively become whoever we wish to be, astronaut, mystic or (my personal favorite) cheese-dog salesman...

NEVER feel guilty about masturbation. If YOU can't touch you, WHO can?

There's not much more I can say about this tenet which has been agreed upon by psychologists, physiologists and even modern theologians. Perhaps I can remind the reader to do two things: use sufficient amounts of lubrication and pick a private place to most comfortably exercise your consummate sexual right...

NEVER trust mirrors. Sometimes they tell you you're beautiful and sometimes they don't. Forebrains and lights have a funny way of manipulating mirrors.

Mirrors are two-dimensional, you on the other hand, are three dimensional. This alone should make mirrors suspect; but, there's far more to the reflection story. First, (psychologically speaking,) how we feel about ourselves (relatively positive or negative) acutely effects how we perceive ourselves (that's right, either positively or negatively.) Second, third and fourth (and of course, physiologically speaking,) facial expressions, glittering eyes and graceful movement are all lost in the frozen pose we (primarily) assume before the looking glass. In short, the person we see over there framed in the mirror is a flat, uninteresting postcard variation of our true self. The 'self' is a complex, both physical and spiritual, three hundred and sixty degree personage who casts many reflections. However, none of these reflections (even that of a three hundred and sixty degree hologram) can ever exist as a unified whole; they are merely images, light refractions which beam off surfaces without probing any real depth. One day, they will create detailed cyborgs and androids which appear totally human in every imaginable way. Nevertheless, these creatures too, will reveal their absolute inhumanity in a staggering number of strangely subtle ways. Simply because they too, (like the mirrors of today,) will   not possess the perfect soul and imperfect bearing of man... Like it or not, man is unique; you and I are odd, peculiar critters. Hence, when we ask the mirror on the wall, "Who's the fairest of them all?", will we answer the loaded question correctly? (Well??..).

BUY candles for your home. Fire is very comforting to humans and you'll be conserving energy; but, try not to burn your house down.

Before human beings mastered fire we were routine snacks for a whole slew of predators with uncommonly bad taste. Naturally, after the harnessing of fire, all that changed. It was only a matter of time before we were wheeling around flame throwers and selling surcharge incendiary weapons to depressed third-world countries while working on our own thermonuclear assault ships five thousand times bigger than any predator which ever chewed our bones. Let's face it, it's time we scaled down the whole FIRE process. A few, good (non-explosive) candles, placed strategically in and around the home, provide unquestionable sanctity in their own warm, peaceful and demure sort of way. Within this simplicity, the candlelight symbolizes a powerful source of spiritual integrity to both the clergyman and fine-scented White Witch or Wiccan (as she prefers to be called.) In either case, when the power of candlelight is escalated into ritualistic forms of worship, it must be done so with great serenity, absolute humility and a fully charged fire extinguisher: just in case the first two tenets are lacking the minimum resolve required by the SOURCE worshipped...

NEVER get angry at superficial things and you'll find yourself getting angry a whole lot less.

We all agree that social existence is an elaborate, melodramatic, and at best surrealistic, caricature of human idealism. Perfection eludes us like supermodels at the annual good old boy picnic. We have come to understand each other by the relative level of annoyance we are freely willing to offer one another. In this ill-adapted madness of everyday life, it's no wonder we find ourselves irritated by the mere sight of each other on the streets of NYC. We continually struggle to better ourselves, to narrow our margin of error and master the intricate performance of our own individualism. Yet, we have no real support structure. All we run into are feeble-minded, imperfect, (and in most cases) drooling homosapiens, in other words, other human beings, just like ourselves. How can we expect perfection in an imperfect body which functions daily in an imperfect society existing upon an imperfect world? Check it out, we can't. So get yourself a modicum of human tolerance and leave the whining to the sheep and the howling to the wolves...

CONVERSELY, don't be afraid to get angry when it becomes absolutely necessary. Anger is a successful survival strategy. However, sometimes you just have to back down, or you may find yourself dead in somebody's trunk.

Never corner an animal unless you are prepared to weather its full-blooded retaliatory attack. Animals instinctively understand Step 61, whether squirrel, cat or hippopotamus, most creatures on God's good earth will strike out when no alternative form of escape is possible. Now, in the mean society created by human beings, we find many and diverse levels of this same aggressive behavior. Fortunately, this nicely layered diversity of behavior blocks us from physically striking out at each other (most of the time.) We have the luxury to exchange harsh glances, argue, yell, scream, curse, throw social and/or economic weight around, create political scandals and reveal secrets to enemy forces. In lieu of this prism of aggressive behavior, we are (somewhat) expected to hold our own ground in society and not be mistaken for easy prey by anyone, anywhere, any time. We restate, however, their are irrefutable times when the higher and highest levels of aggression will come into play. If possible, save these occasions for the police, army or those even better equipped for that particular 'class' of confrontation.

NEVER give up individual rights. Never attack the freedoms given to you by the First Amendment. Never attack the First Amendment.

Hey, freedom is not overrated. In America, we may still be slaves of an economic and two-tiered political order, but as individuals we also possess the freedom to say and write exactly what we feel about that order and damn near anything else which immediately disturbs us. We can (as they say) express our minds, regardless of how vividly enlightened or absurdly moronic our ideas may be. This liberated front of ideas quickens the pulse of the so-called 'democratic' society. It keeps us alive and progressive and challenges those fanatic, fascistic forces who would wish to silence (WE...) the people. Contrary to popular opinion, our puritanical forefathers had very little foresight. They envisioned a world where future religion and faith would be persecuted by intolerant, tyrannical leadership. Instead, we live in a world where a religious, repressive, moral right seeks to persecute a majority of our modern forms of expression and eliminate our so-called 'inalienable' rights. In short, our forefathers blundered correctly and saved us from the stringent ideals of their own moralist traditions. We need to support the good fortune which political fate has bestowed upon us each and every day, and most especially that day so aptly called: Independence Day!

IF your particular religion limits certain freedoms then so be it. YOU CHOSE THE RELIGION, NOW LIVE BY IT. Leave people WHO DID NOT CHOOSE YOUR RELIGION alone. They have to live by their own beliefs.

Individual freedom means individual freedom. Freedom cannot be freedom if it imposes limitations upon others. Liberty must be absolute. Now, liberty is not merely the name of a statue or a national concept (which coincidentally, both carry inoperative torches,) liberty is a product of our divine creation and slow, unravelling evolution. We are a species formed from boundless time into conscious, free-thinking beings capable of reason, choice and the perseverance to uphold our liberated ideals and realistic decisions made. In other words, both God and Nature have given mankind an undeniable freedom of choice. It is the metaphysical plan for each and every human being to decide for him or herself what is right and wrong in accordance with his or her own experience and (intimate?) thought process. What this really means is Man (as a singular creation) is particularly and exceptionally free. Man is a free being. This absolutely reserves all judgement of man's behavior to a force greater than man himself. In short, judgement is reserved for man's creator. This may be the reason why virtually every culture in existence, (today as well as in ancient times,) all depict a clear-cut model of an afterlife, a paradise. If you're good, you make it inside, but if you're bad, well...you don't. Some religions elaborate on this final restriction from paradise due to a lack of GENERAL morality. They envision the immediate entrance into a sort of anti-paradise, that realm called: well, you know...Hell! The point is God is already ON TOP of the situation. No zealots and fanatics are required or desired to enforce HIS universal laws. He is (as they say) all-power-ful and all-knowing. He'll do with the world and its inhab-itants WHATEVER He pleases. To the movers and shakers I say: You do your job of being good, and He'll do HIS job of seeing if you (really are) being good... What could be simpler?

WALK around your neighborhood. Get to know where you live. If you live in a neighborhood where you can't freely get around, for whatever reason, either work to change it, or MOVE!

Everyone knows we cannot allow crime to make us prisoners in our own homes. To assist the police (or WHO-EVER represents the GOOD guys,) we need to create community watches, anonymous tip lines and other security-minded social applications. Simply put: victimizing criminals deny freedom and therefore, they waive a good deal of their own freedoms. Conversely, as fairly socialized and (more or less) non-violent creatures, we have the absolute right to get out and enjoy the streets we pay taxes to keep intact. Every village, town and big city has its own unique character and quirky appeal. Moreover, our environment reflects ourselves. Accordingly, as we certainly cannot give up on ourselves, we also cannot give up on the streets in which we live. Naturally, the problem of poverty and crime is rampant and complex. However, it is not (as they say) out of control. It takes time, patience and the ability to care about our neighbors as much as ourselves. For those of us who couldn't be bothered, (well, tough luck for all of us,) because crime...is an equal opportunity offender. What exists over there, also exists over HERE. We can, however, help each other maintain a slightly higher quality of life; that is, if we really want it. (IF NOT, then (as some suggest) we should affix our best bullet-proof vests, strap on grand-daddy's trusty holsters, sharpen our best Ginzu carving knives, grease the (strictly rental) tech nines, and with hot, reissue WW2 grenades in hand, we can all play the planet Tombstone game, until we blast one another into lifeless, clumps of unrecognizable grime...)

NEVER imitate or try to be like anyone else. This is the biggest violation of NATURE in the universe. Even twins are entirely different.

We live in a very obsessive culture. We are obsessed by fascinating people. We have come to believe that somehow, becoming like these fanciful individuals, we will fulfill all that lacks in our own lives. Hence, we have elevated a whole slew of mere mortals into superstars, supermodels and immortal living legends. Society has created a whole host of these role models to provide a sort of slightly variable focal point toward which all of humanity should aim. Not only is this reasoning stupid, childish and morally bankrupt, it is also NUMB, LACKLUSTER AND ENTIRELY INHUMAN. Like it or not, we are all individuals with entire life-times of our own unique experience, and more importantly, we are intelligent enough to STOP playing follow the leader and king of the hill. Naturally, we can enjoy the accomplishments of 'infamous' people without necessarily worshipping them. The fact is, WE DO NOT LIVE IN A VACUUM and we do in fact borrow traits from famous people and from one another too (it's not exactly a crime.) However, it becomes a crime when we begin hating and punishing ourselves because we are so unlike our 'super' ideals. Envy is a deep, ugly painful emotion which stems from our reptilian brains. One animal has meat and eats it with relish, while another has nothing, looks on with envy, and goes hungry. Our obsessive culture programs us to believe we have nothing if we are unlike the 'chosen few'. Instead of providing motivation for the general public, these icons exaggerate human frailty, weakness and suffering. Be yourself and see how fast you stop the madness...

NEVER worry about BEING YOURSELF. In the simple act of being honest, you are being YOURSELF.

You cannot be someone else and you cannot NOT be yourself. Every time you lift your finger you have enacted your 'will' and changed the course of the universe forever. That's just the way it goes. When you follow the reasoning of your mind as closely as you can, you create the pure embodiment of a prime source of life. You can't help it. Life is just happening to you. We suggest you role with it as best as you can utilizing honest intelligence, honest creativity and as much stamina as you can possibly muster. This way, the choices you make will be (in perhaps, an unsettling sort of way, but that's OK,) based on YOUR OWN unique perspective and prerogative and NOT UPON SOMEONE ELSE'S. You will have lived your own life without blame, regret or remorse. You will have done what you felt and reasoned was right because you will have decided (with some measure of 'ballsy' reasoning and reassurance) exactly what you were all about (in the metaphysical sense) and what you were ULTIMATELY meant to be. You were the master of your own Harley-Davidson, downshifting through the long strip of destiny. In the truest sense, the age of the whiners, moaners and finger-pointers will eventually come to an end. Step up to the cutting edge by being your truest self and possessing the wherewithal to take full responsibility for the actions you know you need to make...

REMEMBER, the more you strive for perfection, the less perfection you'll achieve. Perfection is subjective. Perfection is illusion.

Your idea of 'perfection' is not everybody's idea of 'perfection'. One man's 'supermodel' is another man's 'medical experiment in progress'. Plato wrote extensively about 'ideals'; for example, the ideal chair, ideal boat, ideal tree and ideal man. This 'ideal' existed outside of reality and yet created the vision, or outline, which provided a prime focal point for the physical creation. I agree with Plato to a point, however, I view reality as infinitely complex, and therefore, able to withstand an infinite number of variable 'ideals'. I do not attribute one single 'ideal' for each object in existence to a creator (be that God or Nature) who has created free will, individuality and an infinite amount of creativity in thought. 'Free will' absolutely and positively shapes the perception of what is SUPERIOR. The history of art and the world-wide market of goods illustrates this assortment of subjective, yet equally flawless, beauty. This includes the sublime beauty which is often found in the outright nature of pure ugliness. There are times where we attribute great strength and a near immortal quality to the grotesque, please note: gargoyles, Quasimodo, antediluvian protector DEMON MASKS and of course, Marcel Duchamp's famous Dadaist art-work: The Urinal. In short, keep in mind: perfection does exist and may in fact be a noble pursuit, but it's your own pursuit and not someone else's. Hence, until your ready to unveil your magnum opus to the whole wide world, keep your anal retentive 'ideals' all to yourself. Have no fear, we'll all be waiting for the GRAND EXPOSITION with baited breath. I vow to that...

DO not be afraid to shut yourself off from the world when you need to. Privacy is a very necessary ingredient to sanity.

How many times have we said or heard the phrase, "I need some space." Did we wish in these instances for a space capsule nearby in which we could take off, or conversely, in which we could launch SOMEBODY ELSE far off into space? Sure we have, we can all admit it now. Besides, we were completely justified! We had the inalienable right, that is, the Right of Privacy: the right to be left alone. Fortunately, we have this right in America (at least, most of the time) to sit at home all by ourselves and read a book, this book for example, (a rather convenient example for me,) with nobody watching over our shoulders (with any luck at all.) Naturally, the act of reading itself is, (or at least should be,) quite a private matter. It's just the written word and you; the writer, editor, printer, publisher and distributer are all ancient history. It's just you and you alone. Does that scare you? Maybe not, but it scares the hell out of me. Naturally, that's irrelevant. The real point is you can close the book, turn off the TV, kick out your neighbors, relatives and pets and be entirely BY YOURSELF. Once alone, you can (as they say) 'center' yourself, but more importantly, you can do WHATEVER THE HELL you want to do: uncensored, unrestricted and without all those useless value judgements everybody seems to want to place upon everybody else. That's right, go inside and have some good, clean and highly personal fun! We'll all wait outside with baited breath for your return. I vow to that...

NEVER try to change someone you love. If you don't love them exactly as they are, you don't love them.

There is a perception in attempting new relationships that a prospective partner is one who is good 'raw material', which can be shaped and molded into something worthwhile, by the wholly concerned significant other. No wonder Divorce is a booming, multi-multi-billion dollar a year industry. The Doctor Frankenstein approach to interrelationships is not only egomaniacal, self-centered and devilishly selfish, it also presupposes that an outside personage is better equipped to dictate what another individual thinks, feels and believes. (Little wonder so many mindless, co-dependent monsters are created by this society.) For the record: NOBODY is BETTER than anyone else. Every decision is based upon opinion and perception. As such, either meet your partner in the middle-ground of your relative beliefs, or, find someone else. Fortunately, (or unfortunately, depending upon who you ask,) there are billions of human beings on this planet and hundreds of millions of potential mates to choose from. In the spiritual sense, we should learn to love all these people exactly as they are and were born. But who's going do that??? Hence, since we can't all date Mother Teresa and the Dali Lama, we must try our best to choose people we basically like and are relatively attracted to, the rest (as they say) will (painstakingly and with great horror) come easy...

NEVER fear authority figures. Authority figures never like and never trust people they can scare so easily.

Authority figures represent order, or a well thought out and organized plan of socialization. Therefore, as representative leaders, they should be respected for their knowledge and their forthright ability to uphold the best possible order, rule or law. However, in a free society, it is also our right to be able to question the parameters of any outright authority imposed upon us. We have the right of legal representation and due process if we feel we have been treated unfairly by any forces, any time anywhere. Authority figures represent the rules and the order; but, they are in no way and by no means, the rule and order itself. A free society has been fashioned for us wherein certain ethical standards must be adhered to in all cases, IN EVERY SINGLE CASE! Every authority figure has a superior he or she must answer to and all these superiors have ethics boards which they in turn must satisfy. These boards are controlled by government agencies which are run by elected officials which answer to constituents, who are the people themselves (that's absolutely right, you and me.) The internal 'buddy system' has no legal backbone and moreover, if it can be proven, 'preferential action' can become a criminal offence. THESE ARE NOT FAIRY TALES and never let anyone tell you otherwise. However, you are (as a citizen of society) required to be informed, in other words, you must know your rights and be able to stand up for them. Respect and uphold the law of this great free society, at the same time, never let ANYONE abuse this law for their own personal gain. Only base and paltry leaders need be feared, real authority figures are duly respected and work hand in hand with the society they serve their best to empower.

IF someone annoys you and does not realize it, let them know immediately. Don't be afraid to hurt their feelings. Humans are uncanny at picking up each other's negative feelings. So, it's best to get all of that out of the way.

The human brain doubles as a high sensory scanning unit which reacts to diverse (and abnormal) sensations. For example: when we are confronted with the hostile emotions of another human being, the alarm within our perceptual scanning unit rings and triggers several adrenalin rushes which physiologically aid us in our 'fight or flight' reaction formation. On a deeper level, since the scanning unit is so extremely sensitive, emotions (which are not as yet OUTWARDLY EXPRESSED by another) are nevertheless, completely registered within our own brain. We suddenly find ourselves dimly aware of another human being's internal trepidations. However, since we cannot be absolutely certain of the cause and depth of this inner conflict, we psychologically recoil into a defensive position. We begin to question the other person, or worse, ourselves. As this is repeatedly the case in society, we have an informal, yet absolute, right to clarify or justify the focus of all our perceived emotions. A well-adjusted society (if such a thing exists!) requires a window of opportunity to express (and listen to) all concerns, fears and indignations. Without these honest revelations, we create the seeds of paranoia. Ones own bad feelings may be misinterpreted as the bad feelings of others. In solitude, these emotions can lead to increasing levels of alienation, distrust and insecurity. (Just what we need in NYC!) At this stage of the game, the best way to combat negative emotions may require the attainment of spiritual faith (religious preference optional,) which will assure a strong sense of individual place, purpose and ultimately, meaning.

On the Earth   [77]

NEVER think that any ONE HAPPENING will change everything in your life for the better. Even winning the lottery is FAR from a cure-all.

An extended trip to the Greek Islands, winning the lottery, meeting that super-model who finds you fascinating, these are all good things (no agreement necessary!) However, strange as it may seem, pleasure (see above examples,) comes from within. Our bodies swell out in (endorphin-charged) ecstasy at our own beck and call, each time we choose to exercise the (no holds barred) pleasure of existence. Sufi mystics (and other near-east shaman,) view each breath taken as an absorption of God, conversely, each heart beat is a focus prayer to that same all-powerful creator. Siberian monks also master this concept of the eternal prayer which repeats with each successive 'beat' of the divine heart. In the west, we find internal elation in the union of our physical bodies and spiritual souls (as they reinforce each other) in action, merit and motivation. All around the world, we deliberately create the person(s) we need to become in order to gain our highest sense of fulfillment. Modern theory agrees that Individualism (which provides that most SUBLIME sense of FREEDOM) is not given, (not handed out from a platter,) it is rather a slow mastery which develops over a long period of time and with some degree of visceral torture. As we develop as individuals, we find the real pleasure found in the creation, realization and fullest attainment of self. On the other hand, Sufi mystics never had supermodels either...

ON CHILDREN: SURROUND a very young child's play area with what you consider to be meaningless, harmless objects. Let the child decide if he wants them or not. He may want some and not others. Do not question why.

There is a great deal of truth in 'a priori' creativity. In other words, we are by and large born with our creative gifts (art, music, tunnel excavation...) Nonetheless, these gifts (or lack of them!) expand one hundred-fold with stages of self-learning, hand in hand, with self-experimentation. An infant's mind is assembling billions of neural cell connections at blinding speeds. As such, his perceptual powers are developing quicker and more efficiently than at any other point in his entire life. Consequently, the child's experimentation and manipulation (RIGHT NOW!) plays an astronomical role in how he or she will perceive the outside world and its relative cerebral effect. In this sense, a child's adaptive 'a priori' mind is simultaneously classifying and clarifying reality each and every time he places his wee, little hands on all new physical stimuli. We're not saying that if the infant is given a toy boat he will automatically become the captain of a nuclear aircraft carrier; but we are saying that a child may contemplate the concepts of floatation, movement and some of the elemental principles of water, better with the toy boat, than without. The point of surrounding a child's play area with safe, noningestive objects, is that the child will transfigure the shape, texture and relative hardness of these objects in neuro-cellular synapses which are incomprehensible to the parent or professional researcher. The child is creating and augmenting himself (not entirely unlike 'The Blob' in Steve McQueen's first cinematic outing.) In years to come, this initial creative formation cultivated within the child's mind will underline a large part of his or her crucial decision making. Hence, instead of saying, 'Spare the rod, spoil the child.' we may instead need to say, 'Spare the block, spoil the engineer...'

ON CHILDREN: YOU are still a child: never let the adult world get you down. Children learn best from other children. You are that 'other' child.

We are all of us learning, growing and gradually aging (except for hollywood actresses who morph into tiny-muscle endowed, cyborgesque humanoids.) In any case, our ongoing development makes us differ minimally from our children. The difference between adults and children merely lies in their comparative rates of growth. Adults are a bit slower, even those of us who jog ten miles a day in rain, heat or snow. As such, children instinctively understand (that) we adults are merely slower versions of themselves. We can partially be trusted. If we stop barking commands and start interacting with our children instead, we may begin to understand the real meaning of 'childhood'. Theirs, as well as OUR OWN. Let's face it, to be 'full grown', may just mean you're dead. To grow no more...

NEVER let your EGO get in the way of trying something new. Never worry about failure. Failure is subjective. Failure is illusion.

Some people say, 'When in Rome, do as the Romans.' Sure thing. But first, you have to get to Rome. This may require bus, train, helicopter or super-sonic transport (depending on your relative orientation.) Once you arrive in Rome, you immediately need to figure out what to wear, where to go and who to be seen with. This is singularly because, as cultural beings, most of us are terrified at the prospect of 'standing out' in society. We feel the need to fit into every single community we find ourselves thrust within. Our seemingly all-powerful egos shrivel away at the thought of receiving any ridicule or public humiliation, whatsoever. Hence, we MUST become acting romans in order to smoothly blend into the analogous world-scheme of Rome. Naturally, all too many people are concerned (scared excrementless you might say!) about their capability to 'romanize' quickly, or accordingly enough, to make the grade in Rome. Consequently, they give up on the whole idea and remain seated in their comfortable living rooms in Piscataway, N.J. Having been to Piscataway and loving it immensely (sarcasm optional,) I can safely state that a trip to Rome, Paris, Thailand, London, Lisbon, Sydney, Athens, Portugal, Brazil, Los Angeles and even good old N.Y.C. (the latter a simple trip over the G.W. bridge from Piscataway) can be a highly worthwhile experience. As such, we see how and why the overcoming of social fear is an absolute necessity in the highest fulfillment of everyday life. We say, 'When in Rome, forget the romans and do whatever the hell it is you usually do!' Notwithstanding the Pope, the romans are fairly open- minded folk...

HOWEVER, always focus your concentration on the most potentially dangerous situation at any given moment.

In a dangerous situation (for example: being nearly run over by the Pope-mobile) you'll find that time seems to slow down to a snail's pace (sort of the reverse of the adage, 'time flies when you're having fun'.) In these long, slow moments of hyper-awareness it is not difficult to focus on the very real reality of a threatening force. With some measure of composure (and certainly without panic) you may be able to properly assess a viable way out of a dangerous situation. For example, a New Yorker (and a roman too, no doubt) both instinctively know not to stare down a gang of violent youths scanning (bloody!) mischief. If their 'minding my own business' approach yields no results, awareness and reason help them coordinate another way of avoidance (or casual escape!) If there is simply no way out (for example: the Pope-mobile has the roman cornered in an alley) some form of assurance of his non-threatening presence may become absolutely and immediately necessary (sometimes this may simply entail remaining silent, or pious, in the case of the high revving Pope-mobile.) Having failed all of the above, straight forward and firm negotiations may be all that's left to him; however, at this point he should be prepared for the worse possible scenario (still, believe it or not, without panic.) A quick surveillance of his protagonists weak points may remove the normal 'freezing' aspect of reactionary fear, which at this point, can only be detrimental to him. He must keep in mind the ancient roman adage, 'Know thine enemy.' In the case of the Pope, he may be in over his head...

NEVER be caught off guard by anyone or anything. If you ARE caught off guard, do not freeze, instead, move slowly and confidently in the direction of the danger.

It is paramount to stay 'cool' and 'aware' in novel environments. Criminals have a way of preying on those of us who appear disorientated, unsure, or otherwise oblivious. Have several names of friends and acquaintances immediately popped in your head? These folks may need to be told (right now, rush to the phone if you have to) that only with a confident and straightforward demeanor will most of the potentially dangerous factors surrounding them be immediately eliminated. In the same way, an enemy who catches them (or us) off guard, must be confronted right then and there. To become entirely helpless before a violent protagonist will (more often than not) lead to dire consequences. In this sense, it is crucial for rape victims to scream, kick, bite and forcefully challenge their assailant. Moreover, the victim should never, ever allow the assailant to push them into a car and drive them off to some remote or isolated location. The victim is far better off causing a traffic accident (which may alert police) by kicking out a gear box, window, brake pedal or kneecap. If this fails, the importance of knowing ones enemy is paramount in understanding the motivation of their violent behavior. For example: if an assailant enjoys overpowering his victims in a sadistic fashion, an astute victim may frustrate him by remaining motionless and utterly corpse-like. In all cases the victim must remain aware, knowledgeable and exercise the best possible judgement (whether that be a sock in the jaw. or a kind word about the assailant's daddy serving time in a tiny prison cell.) Never forget: every human mind is utterly complex, even, and sometimes especially, THE CRIMINAL MIND.

Seaburn Survival Series   *[84]*

IN combat, react to any 'quick' movement toward you with an equally 'quick' movement in an alternate direction. If you cannot react fast enough, relax your muscles upon impact.

I know, I know, this sounds a whole lot easier than it actually may be. However, all aspects of life possess a reasonable cause and effect mechanism and therefore can be learned (at least on some superficial level.) In the course of physical confrontation we generally depend on four physiological factors: balance, flexibility, speed and force. A flurry of unbalanced smacks and swats expend crucial energy and will have very little real effect on an assailant (who is expecting this sort of chaotic struggle anyway.) However, sharp, well-aimed kicks, punches (using the lower base of the palm, rather than the closed fist) and swift, evenly aligned elbow jabs will yield far better results to all those brave enough to try them. Naturally, physical training such as karate, high-impact aerobics and gymnastics aid in the proper focus and coordination required in all forms of self-defence. For those of us who are unable to practice these methods of physical mastery, simple self-defence courses for beginners are offered and available in nearly town and city in the known world (consult your local yellow pages.) Having done so, take this little piece of advice I once read on a billboard somewhere in the heart of USA: 'Don't be frightened, be enlightened!'

NEVER let FEAR bring you to the point where you are OUT OF CONTROL in a dangerous situation. Stay fit and aware.

As in all of the previous examples of dangerous situations, the paramount rule was always to remain calm and never panic. Naturally, since fear is a deeply seated biological instinct, we cannot simply erase it by concentrating our sheer force of will. What we can do, however, is limit and gradually decrease its overall effect upon us. This can initially be achieved by coordinating certain principles of our body, mind and spirit. In reverse order, beginning with our spiritual sense; we must keep faith in our purposeful existence by remembering our God (or other Spiritual Guide) is on our side, and therefore, protects us in a myriad of incomprehensible ways. Secondly, we have reason and awareness (rational mind) which will compel us to make intelligent, sound choices which will further insure our safety. Lastly, we can slow down our (bodily) heart rate through meditation and deep breathing techniques which will prepare our bodies for any and all appropriate responses dictated by mind and strengthened by faith. In short, the combination of faith, reason and meditation, will begin reducing the paralyzing effect of fear, which does us no good whatsoever. After all, are we Bambi, frozen in the oncoming headlights of existence?!!

STAYING fit essentially narrows down to three factors: Digestible intake, Amount of digestible intake and Amount of energy expended after digestible intake.

Returning our attention to the physical body in its normal state of affairs, we find a fluid, purposeful machine which demands a certain (quality and quantity of) matter intake to function and perform at optimum capability. Simply stated, the body wants FOOD and DRINK it can actually USE (that is to say, food and drink it can break down and absorb,) but, NOT TOO MUCH OF IT! The human body is fantastically efficient; it can utilize a glass of orange juice and a cup of yogurt for hours on end. Conversely, eating a seven course meal topped off by a scrumptious liquor mint, foolishly weighs down and overloads the entire system. Would you use a whole box of detergent to wash one load of laundry? (By the way, if you answer that question in the affirmative, don't tell the environmentalists. Because they'll hunt you down like a dog.) I'm hoping the answer is, 'Of course I don't, you bloody idiot!' Fabulous. In that case, don't overload your own system like a dang fool either. (Reminder from the bloody idiot: this advice does not exclusively apply to the obese or 'portly' people among us, it applies to ALL of the over-indulgent, gluttonous folk lurking silently in the crowd below...) The pious person who once told us that gluttony was one of the seven deadly sins (an ancient Jane Fonda?) had, without a doubt, an extremely legitimate point about self-abuse. All this, and we haven't even taken GLOBAL FAMINE into account, (yet...) Bon appetite!

ALWAYS eat foods that ELIMINATE completely. Avoid foods that stay in your intestines and colon. Most of the nutritious foods like yogurt, bran, vegetables, fruit and small portions of meat will eliminate completely AND are high in vitamins.

O.K. What goes in must come out (or at least a good part of it!) When the body is functioning properly it utilizes proteins and other nutrients and eliminates waste. Yes, that's EXACTLY what I just finished writing down: THE BODY ELIMINATES WASTE. Waste is called waste because it is waste and the INTELLIGENT body does not want this waste (or fecal matter) hanging around! In fact, it works very hard to get rid of it. Unfortunately, some foods create waste that simply refuse to leave the body by using unnatural glycogen secretions to anchor into the body. Day in and day out, the waste of these junk foods just love to hang around, clogging up arteries, organs and fatty tissue. You know the type. Like neighbors who never leave (even after the last video is long over and done with!) Eat healthy and you invite useful, well-mannered guests (eliminative foods) into your real home (that would be the stomach.) Eat unhealthy and you've invited useless miscreants who want to spray paint the carpet, walls and halls of your entire digestive tract. The choice seems so simple until you come face to face with a little, chocolate donut, right?...

ALWAYS eat when you're hungry. Never eat when you're not hungry.

Notwithstanding Pavlovian conditioning, where the body is trained by behavior modification (be it a bell or a Taco Bell commercial) to salivate on command, the body generally knows and can communicate its best needs. The real 'body language' is desire (hunger, fatigue, thirst, arousal, etc.) This is how the body speaks to the mind: simple, direct and without fanfare (the chaotic dance of neuro-transmitters upon myelin sheets notwithstanding.) As disciplined thinkers, we can alter our bodies needs, however, we in no way can replace the ongoing communications of body and mind. It simply isn't done. Fortunately, the mind does best in attaining the required nourishment of the bodies desires, be it oat bran, a new mate, or a new Porsche (for tired feet?) In fact, the mind only fails when it begins ignoring the body. Then we become Star Trek brain pods, programmable eunuchs, ascetics without sustenance, hypnotized beings without expression and finally, sixteenth-century Puritans, all over again. We must ask ourselves, would we really want this to happen? Again?

ALWAYS be active, even if that means the simple act of taking slow strolls down the boulevard humming to yourself.

Life is an act of faith which propels itself forward into the miraculous performance of being. (Don't worry, we're not sure what that means either.) Suffice to say, when all movement stops: movement of body, movement of mind and especially movement of spirit, all of life is lost. There are no other words, life simply BECOMES NO MORE. The very essence of what we are is framed, outlined and utterly determined by the actions we take. In this sense, the only way to expand and grow in what is truly a limited life span (after all, we can't all be George Burns,) is to remain active in the united worlds of bodily animation, mental creativity and spiritual conviction (whether we find our power source with God or a friendly swarm of fire ants.) Hence, we can't just sit around and wait for life to happen to us, we have to go out and generate life's pulse FOR OURSELVES. Furthermore, we need to consider doing these things BEFORE all activity is nullified for us in our most untimely of deaths, when they have no choice but to sullenly bury us under a bulky stone, warmer in touch than our own skin...(!)

NEVER worry about other people's reactions to your physical body. Their reactions are subjective. Their reactions are illusion.

Would you go to an art museum which featured only one pretty painting, repainted over and over again, to fill the entire hall? Similarly, would you enjoy walking through a forest filled with only one species of trees, varying ever so slightly, one from another? Maybe you would. (Some of us get extremely hot and bothered when thinking about absolute uniformity; military generals have a habit of behaving like that...) Whatever floats your boat and keeps you from jumping off tall buildings in a single bound, that's what I maintain! Most of us, however, enjoy the wide variety which a forest offers, from twisted shrunken trees to multi-colored towering giants. In much the same way, we like to see our art museums reflecting the full spectrum of diversity found in man's nightmarish, enlightened and wholly unpredictable vision. The human brain searches for variety to stimulate its most elaborate perceptive 'hardware'. As such, beauty is effectively subjective. Each of us are drawn into our own concept of comeliness and grace. We each perceive lines and curves, shades and textures in our own unique and dynamic way. And really, shouldn't it be like that? Nature proves again, it does know best.

ALWAYS listen to YOUR BODY, deep down, only YOUR BODY knows what's good for it.

Earlier, we spoke about the body communicating, or 'speaking to' the mind. In most cases the message is loud and clear, "I'm hungry! Feed me now or double over with my displeasure for the rest of the night!" However, the human body is not a fragile 'cry baby' and therefore, it will not always cry out for its less pertinent needs and relative concerns. Instead, the body will offer 'suggestions' and hints about oncoming sickness and infirmity. This communication is generally known in medical terms as a 'symptom'. Unfortunately, we don't all have specialists and doctors camping out in our living rooms. (They probably would ignore us if we didn't have medical coverage, anyway. Living room or not.) Therefore, we need to take the time necessary to LEARN ABOUT OUR OWN BODIES in order to listen to their 'suggestions' with the greatest degree of accuracy possible. With the ability to listen closely to our bodies, we can spear-head a great deal of future concerns. (Did I just write spear-head??) Conversely, if we ignore the bodies' hints and wait until it ultimately cries out for help (which as we've seen, it really doesn't want to do,) chances are it will already be too late (though we can't say the body didn't try to warn us with all those massive hints and suggestive symptoms!) And then what happens? You guessed it: all the doctors and specialists and all the kings horses and all the kings men won't be able to put us back together, ever again... Ooooops!

REMEMBER separate physical bodies in human beings, apart from their mental processes, remain individual and unique unto themselves.

We agree with the maxim which states that all men are created equal, however, the equanimity of our beginning source (God's primal soup!) does not singularly categorize the uniformity of our sameness as human beings. The complexity of our individual genetic codes compliment the modern infinite-probability theories of quantum physics. In other words, (God?) has created each and every one of us in such a way, that each of us are absolutely distinctive beings, right down to our tiniest, sub-atomic particles. (Perhaps for his own divine experimentation?) Regardless, physiologically speaking, we are in many ways the multiple faces of God, every line, crease and texture an allusion to the all-encompassing creation. We are as physical beings, far more unique than even our 'cutting edge' modes of expression. Each of us bares distinct marks and mechanisms which separate us from every other being ever born. One day, even clones will develop unique to their specific experience. In lieu of all this (perhaps sickening!) uniqueness, we must consider the biological division of our corporal bodies. We are not quite like our neighbors, friends, or even our relatives. Food, medication and environmental conditions acutely effect us in ways WHICH ONLY WE can discover for ourselves. As such, we MUST tell our physicians, nutritionists, psychologists, personal trainers, grocery clerks, and masseuses which 'samples' of offered assistance yield good (or not so good!) results to our specific experience. If they don't listen, immediately cancel their business association. After all, this IS America, land of the second, third AND fourth opinions...

NEVER stop discovering yourself. Even the most minute things which you will certainly learn about yourself, mean a lot and add up to a lot. Never stop creating yourself.

Contrary to the opinion of many post-apocalyptic, self-destructive types (who take Freud's Death-Instinct theory far too seriously,) perception is not a curse, but rather a prize gift. Even when the perception is dark, grizzly and grotesque (sometimes PRIMARILY when the perception is dark, grizzly and grotesque,) we assimilate the human condition in dual measure with the fragile, mortal transience of worldly existence. When we internalize the perceived imperfection of self, we contemplate the real purpose of kindness, merit and above all, forgiveness. Goodness develops as a direct response to EVIL (and vice-versa!) The coin always has two sides. As such, as we continuously learn about ourselves, we will no doubt witness successive stages of our own best and worst 'qualities'. We need to come to terms with this complexity which is in fact, our own SIGNIFICANT humanity. When we hide from the truth of ourselves we lose the WHOLE experience of SELF. Do we want to be HALF the men we used to be, as the song suggests? Moreover, why should we wax and wane, when we can always be FULL MOONS. We should discover ourselves and reveal ourselves, right here and right now, because there's no-one quite like us in the entire universe (and Amen to that!)

IF your way of life does not LIMIT others, then never let anyone LIMIT yours, including yourself. Do it above and beyond the call of duty.

Within the jurisdiction of law, decency and dignity (good taste optional,) push yourself (that is to say, your wildest visions) as far as they can possibly go. Unless you aggressively 'push the envelope', you will never discover the absolute potential of your desire, action and will. Even the serenity of monks is shaped on the hard discipline which fuses sublime faith and the deterministic will necessary to surrender oneself to a spiritual way of life. However, (not entirely unlike some [not so devout] monks, masters and missionaries,) as we set goals for ourselves, we (more often than not) create our own limitations and barriers to slow us down. These psychological limitations, blocks or walls serve us no real purpose, UNTIL, we can understand and over-come (hurdle) their presence. As such, we must come to terms with the reason for their emotional existence within us. We must examine ourselves and the valid stages of our own development. What went wrong, and why? It is only natural these wayward, off-course journeys of our past would figure prominently into the headings of our possible futures. Yet, without the realization and overcoming of these personal barriers, we would continuously find ourselves adrift in the ancient mires of our own murky past. Can we allow our future headings to be effected by maps penned so long ago in our experience? Find faith, seek professional help and buy all the NEW maps you can possibly get your hands on, but refuse to let your PAST get in the way of your FUTURE. Life is too short...

EVERY so often, stop and think about where you are, who you are and why you are.

The journey through life entails an ever changing course (whether you're a high-seas adventurer or a traffic cop whose worked the same intersection for some thirty-nine years.) Existence has its fair share of upheavals for all of us. ERGO, as we travel down this road of life we should, every now and then, examine our relative condition and position. Are we the same person we used to be yesterday, last year, or thirty-nine years ago? If not, how have we changed and how have we stayed the same? (Well?!!) Has the world around us changed? If so, do we perceive it as being better, or worse? (Well?!!) Are our actions today leading us toward our best possible tomorrows? (Are they?!! These are fairly important questions.) The point is, a moment of self-reflection is always in order, before we re-enter the super highway of life. Will we run out of gas? Are our headlights on? Is that a herd of bloody caribou charging in our direction?!! (The reader can omit the latter if they absolutely feel the need to edit out my slightly paranoid imagery...)

NEVER answer the question 'WHY YOU ARE?' unless you're someone like me, who loves to think in riddles. The Divinity is most certainly a riddle, one way or the other.

In a logical sense, the existential question 'why?' is best saved for some form of creator, however, unlike the questions who?, where?, how? and what?, the question 'why?', sometimes clearly answers itself. For example, if I create a box, I have done so in order to utilize a box. Why? I want to hold or store some object, which a box, does best. I did not create a shoe, telephone or magnetic hairbrush. Those things are useful, but not for holding or storage. I offer a further example. Why do I paint my house? So that my house will have a fresh coat of paint, in short, it will be painted. I did not paint my house to clean my house, or to rid my house of ants. I use cleansers and exterminators for that. Taking this argument to the next level, we may ask why has God (or evolution) created human beings? To me the answer is quite simple. Human beings were created to provide humanity. Nature couldn't depend on moths, wooly mammoths or giant sea snakes to do the work of man. For better or worse, man exists to represent himself in the brilliant, ongoing scheme of reality. Keep that in mind the next time you're contemplating doing something stupid!

REMEMBER, every object on earth has a definite sensitivity that can 'pick up' human emotions on their own level. So, as often as you can, try to 'feel good' around the objects all around you. They just may return the favor.

Physicists as philosophically diverse as Einstein and Heisenberg have equally illustrated how matter consists of fields of energy which take on form, shape and texture. Hence, the physical world around us is in constant motion. (Not to worry, unless you've been drinking Alabama Slammers all night, you probably won't fall down.) That motion, (of matter, not the alabama slammers,) be it random or selective, [see: step 1], radiates a sub-atomic particle/wavelength which provides the very substructure of material existence. (No real reason to start [or stop!] drinking. But anticipate more...) Furthermore, (see, I thought so,) since this matter is pure energy, it can neither be created or destroyed, merely transformed. This strongly suggests that energy has always been around, plans to stay around, and basically, knows exactly what its doing. (Can you say: 'Master Plan?') This inbred 'intelligence' of energy reveals its 'innate' interaction. In other words, all wavelengths of energy act together and form a relative alliance. ONLY NOW, can we get to the point! The highly complex, organ-stuffed human body (drinking alabama slammers or not,) is itself an extremely powerful and influential source of this same particle/wavelength energy. Practitioners of telekinesis, (people who bend matter merely by concentrating upon it,) Kung Fu martial artists, (98 pound men who effortlessly smash many slabs of CONCRETE with their open hand,) fire-walkers, fire-swallowers and even fire-fighters, all demonstrate the incredible flexibility and force of our (energized) bodies. Consequently, even us ordinary folk, can 'sense' and in turn 'effect', the entire world around us. (And you thought it was the Alabama Slammers which possessed the strange force!)

ALWAYS take pleasure in your actions, no matter how mundane.

Step 94 is really an extension of step 93. It refers to our human 'extension' into the waiting environment. Like Midas, we possess a touch of gold which can either make or break the world around us. The force of our internal and limitless resources absolutely resounds upon the integrity of our surrounding material universe. In other words, unlike any other creature ever born, us human things, I mean beings, have an almost surreal ability to project our internal emotions upon the living background of our own reality. We can transform hunks of glue, sand and pigment into works of art which warm, excite and transcend souls for generations to come. We can do our best to save a species from extinction and televise the whole event for posterity. We can fling projectiles into the orbit of nearby planets and foresee cohabitation with alien cultures who might just desire the same (for whatever reason!) We can visualize and dream and express our dreams and visions in technicolor splendor. We can even maintain hope and express sarcasm simultaneously! CONTRARY to the words of the ever resplendent Brian Gyson, 'Man is NOT a bad animal!' Step 94 reminds us of our polished side!

TRY to appreciate your complete range of emotions and awareness. When you learn to admire your ability to react to the outside world, then your outlook on the outside world will deepen and gain meaning.

When we come to terms with our own humanity and human potential, we will then fully adapt the vision of the countless visionaries and prophets who have come before us. When we understand the finest purpose of our existence centers around our own self-knowledge, then our actions (premeditated or otherwise) will work for the common (and uncommon!) good of all. (Admittedly, big shoes to fill RIGHT NOW.) However, as time takes its course, we will gradually step into the calm of our own mythology and piece by piece we will materialize the new dreams necessary to guide us further along on our way. (Am I optimistic, or what?) Remember, we are a comparatively young species and already our effect on the planet has been both remarkable and devastating. Clearly, our potential is no fantasy. It's rather unfortunate so many individuals in society find themselves caught up in the psychological neurosis of self-hatred. Billions of human beings just out in out hate humanity. We'd rather blame and chastise ourselves (or our kind) for unsatisfactory behavior, rather than altering that unsatisfactory behavior. Instead of SUPPORTING creation we feel the need to DESTROY our pitiful lack of creation! What are we? Are we peasants in an old horror flick, carrying torches and screaming for the death of the poor monster, which we ourselves have created? (We are, aren't we..?)

NEVER curse or lose respect for the world around you. Life on Earth can be made easier because life on Earth is a divine happening. Divinity can be, and most likely is, a simple thing that sparkles in perceived complexity. Sit back and enjoy every perception's divine creativity.

There's something to be said about life. Sometimes it can really suck! You can find yourself nose deep in misery simply because life decided to throw one too may curve-balls at your exposed groin, and you, YOU JUST WEREN'T READY FOR IT. Over and over again, you just may find yourself downtrodden and beaten with seemingly nobody in the world to turn to for help. Eventually, you may plainly run out of tears and bite all the pink flesh off your own vulnerable lip. Let's face it, you may even in a maniacal moment of intolerance, lose your very own humanity and blast into the dark, painless void of absolute dementia. There is a kind of absolute dementia lurking in the world of the Unconscious Mind which will allow a person to ERASE his PRIMARY and core WILL TO LIVE. Suicide is an act of will, far beyond all emotion and reason, it is the impulse of a lost soul attacking the vacant body of an all too blunt existence. For that person, the only semblance of a thought construct (at all) is to STOP THE PAIN, once and for all. The end, that's it. BUT, BUT, BUT, (and these are very big buts, pardon the pun,) the end doesn't simply occur right after the beginning. There are so many stages of progression in life, and life, (that same life that we all agree can really suck always has the flip side,) has so many sides, so many angles and quite frankly, so many outs. There are people who dedicate their entire lives to aid the troubled; there are organizations set up simply to get people back on their feet. There are entire spiritual faiths based on giving hope to the hopeless. Life is tough mother (agreed), but a mother nonetheless. She'll never give up on you. So don't give up on her... (Watch a 'Rocky' movie if you have to!)

MATERIALISTICALLY, live as simple and free as you can.

Do we each own and operate hundreds of human bodies, or is it just the one, which we must nurture and come to gradually understand? Similarly, does the monk live in a mansion, or is he better suited for a humble home which he can bless and fill with candle-light each day? Our homes and goods reflect the sanctity of our souls. Have you ever heard a man or woman loudly exclaim, "Now, I have enough!" ? What drives man to 'inherit the earth'? (Is it his B.M.W.?) We don't wish to knock the QUALITY of goods, merely the needless possession of an obscene QUANTITY of goods. Can a man ever be judged by the size of his mountain of gold? (Bare with me, I'm going somewhere with this.) Sadly, many in our society answer all these simple questions 100% INCORRECTLY, and sadder still, until they change their mind-set, all the over-priced therapists in the world simply won't be able to ease their mental anxiety. As we have seen time and time again in the course of this book, animated life is an entirely complex undertaking which entails a life-time of (full-time!) mastery. Why then, would you weigh down an already over-full and quite often arduous, LIFE, with concerns about your warehouses full of shiny possessions which can be lost, stolen or leeched upon, each and every day of your life? The truth is, all our possessions will gladly abandon us at the exact moment when we gasp for that last vital breath of air (which thankfully and mercifully, will be free of charge!)

BATHE your home and body regularly.

We're not suggesting the reader become obsessed with this seemingly purifying step. There is no human being on earth who needs to wash his hands fifty times a day. Similarly, building an air-tight, microbe-proof, chamber of a house (like Howard Hughs tried to do,) is also exceedingly preposterous (and silly, when you come right down to it. We live (and HAVE TO LIVE) within a society laden with all sorts of unfriendly, microscopic parasites. (And I DO mean the germs, bacteria and viral strains, NOT the people!) In truth, our immune systems absolutely require exposure to these infinitesimal, lilliputian villains, simply in order to produce anti-bodies adapted to repel them. (The body produces NO SUCH IMMUNITY for aggravating people.) Not at all, step 98 merely suggests a cleansing approach to personal existence. When the body is cleansed, it immediately becomes psychologically and spiritually liberated. We symbolically (and admittedly, hygienically) begin life anew each day, unmarked, unmarred and unhampered. (Take a shower when you're stressed [or depressed] and observe the very real results.) Concerning house-cleaning, we should know that our home doubles as our PERSONAL and immediate environmental background. When it is well-maintained, sanitary and otherwise uncontaminated, we feel not only untroubled and relaxed, but also CRADLED within the hearth of its confines.

NEVER have children for selfish reasons. Never populate mindlessly.

Human beings love to procreate! Nothing we can say can ever change that single reality. We could go on and on for hours on end warning readers about the overpopulation crisis. But really, we'd hardly expect to see the numbers begin to drop. Humans are what they are! Like every other species, bearing young (reproduction, if you want to call it that!) remains the primary goal of human beings. Realizing all this, we could frozenly lecture for another several hours about the levels of maturity, responsibility and economic stability necessary to raise a child in today's world. We could, we really could. But would people actually listen? And those who did listen, would they fully understand all the implications? Can we really ever expect people to ignore both their emotional AND physiological impulses occurring simultaneously? We have no doubt in our minds, these are difficult questions which will plague us all for a long, long time to come. Consequently, We throw in the towel on this whole procreation affair. (Hold the phone! We're not done yet.) We will nonetheless, support step 99, and sneak in two humble suggestions to all 'would be' parents. #1. Love your children MORE than you love YOURSELF. #2. Admit when your in over your head and SEEK PROFESSIONAL GUIDANCE. (From anywhere in the U.S., its always just a phone call away.) This society will never let your children suffer needlessly. Will you?!! Speak now, or NEVER, EVER withhold your contraception! Ever again...

ALWAYS give yourself 4 or 5 names. Give each of your names a special mission here on Earth. Always let your 5 names help and inspire one another. There is no cheating within oneself, within one world, within one creation.

We have examined the human being. We have witnessed the miraculous (outrage!) of his living potential. We have seen the blinding scorch of his touch, the limitless flight of his sight and the boundless light of his eternal spirit. Now we ask: "How many faces belong to him?" And then we ask: "How many faces belong to you?" (After all, you did know we were referring to YOU [in the fine print] of the pages in this book, didn't you?) Why? Because you're a fine specimen whose image should be carved upon the surface of URANUS, that's the reason why! And that's the same phantasmagorical reason why we chose to write a book about you and your seemingly effortless command of the 100 steps necessary for Survival on the Earth. You do us proud! You do us REAL proud. (Now, FINALLY, you can go put this book away, somewhere squashed up on the shelf with the rest of them, lonely and unwanted...) But before you do, we OFFER you one more Step, a BONUS STEP, free of charge. (Hence, the reference: 'Bonus...')

BONUS STEP

NEVER HAVE Passionate Sex On A Weak Branch Of A Very Tall Tree.

YOU MAY FALL DOWN.

[NOTES]

[NOTES]

[NOTES]

100 STEPS NECESSARY FOR SURVIVAL:

EARTH
COLLEGE
NEW YORK, FOR PEOPLE OF COLOR
ARMY
NURSING HOME
RELATIONSHIP
STRESS ENVIRONMENT
AMERICA, FOR THE IMMIGRANT
NEW YORK PUBLIC SCHOOLS

ASK FOR A SPECIAL SURVIVAL SERIES FOR:

ALASKA
AMSTERDAM
BRUSSELS
CALIFORNIA
CHICAGO
GHANA
GREECE
HUSTON
ISTANBUL
JAMAICA
JAPAN
JERUSALEM
LAGOS
LONDON
LOS ANGELES
MOSCOW
NEWARK
PARIS
WASHINGTON, DC

$4.95 US PER COPY
Add $2.00 per book for Shipping & Handling

Send payment to Seaburn, PO Box 2085, LIC, NY 11102
For Credit Card Orders, call:
(718) 274-1300